"If we're going to do this, we have to move fast. You have to get rid of Sal and Paul. Now. They can't know we're leaving."

Liz shot a troubled glance Adam's way. He was asking her to make a split-second decision. And it wasn't a simple decision. Whatever choice she made would have long-lasting effects on a small boy's life.

She had always run things by the book, followed the rules just as her father had taught her. No one would ever expect her to sanction this idea—and that might be the very reason it could work.

Adam's eyes locked with hers in an intense, steady stare. "Trust me."

Trust him?

Dear Lord, I trusted him once with my heart and he shattered it into a million pieces. Do I dare trust him again—this time with my life...and the life of that innocent child? Help me make the right decision, Lord.

Liz looked at Adam and nodded. "Let's do it."

Books by Diane Burke

Love Inspired Suspense

Midnight Caller
Double Identity
Bounty Hunter Guardian
Silent Witness

DIANE BURKE

is the mother of two grown sons and the grandmother of three wonderful, growing-like-weeds grandsons. She has two daughters-in-law who have blessed her by their addition to her family. She lives in Florida, nestled somewhere between the Daytona Beach speedway and the St. Augustine fort, with Cocoa, her golden Lab, and Thea, her border collie. Thea and Cocoa don't know they are dogs, because no one has ever told them. Shhh.

When she was growing up, her siblings always believed she could "exaggerate" her way through any story and often waited with bated breath to see how events turned out, even though they had been present at most of them. Now she brings those stories to life on the written page.

Her writing has earned her numerous awards, including a Daphne du Maurier Award of Excellence.

She would love to hear from her readers. You can contact her at diane@dianeburkeauthor.com.

SILENT WITNESS

DIANE BURKE

Love Inspired

Recycling programs for this product may not exist in your area.

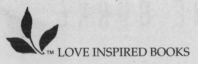

™ LOVE INSPIRED BOOKS

ISBN-13: 978-0-373-44503-5

SILENT WITNESS

Copyright © 2012 by Diane Burke

This edition published by arrangement with Love Inspired Books.

® and TM are trademarks of Love Inspired Books, used under license. Trademarks indicated with ® are registered in the United States Patent and Trademark Office, the Canadian Trade Marks Office and in other countries.

www.LoveInspiredBooks.com

Printed in U.S.A.

For every child of God defeats this evil world,
and we achieve this victory through our faith.
—*1 John* 5:4

My sincerest thanks to my wonderful editors,
Sarah McDaniel-Dyer and Tina James.
They go the extra mile to make my work
the best it can be. I am truly blessed.

ONE

The person who coined the phrase "you can't go home again" apparently forgot to tell Adam Morgan.

Sheriff Elizabeth Bradford tossed the remnants of her half-eaten sandwich to the ducks and wished she could figure out a way to avoid running into him. She'd rather have a root canal without Novocain, or break up a barroom brawl. She'd buried this chapter of her life. Was it too much to wish it would have stayed buried?

Liz watched the Missouri residents pass by from her spot on the park bench. Children played on swings and hung from monkey bars. Owners walked their dogs. People rested under trees reading books or they huddled together having quiet conversations. Everything appeared like any normal summer day—except it wasn't, was it?

Adam Morgan was back in town.

Her stomach clenched.

This was crazy.

They broke up over fifteen years ago. She'd put it behind her and moved on, or at least that's what she kept telling herself.

The radio transmitter on Liz's shoulder crackled and

the dispatcher's voice called out her personal identification code. "Bravo 24."

Liz rose and headed toward her patrol car. Putting her personal issues aside and, in full sheriff mode, she hit the transmit key on her shoulder.

"Bravo 24. Go ahead."

"Code 187. Location 145 Creek Trail."

She stopped abruptly. Her heart skipped a beat. Double homicides? Here? Nothing ever happened here. Nothing bad, that is.

Sure, they had some problems with drugs. All towns did. Their first drug-related homicide had happened just last week. A small-time dealer was murdered and his body left in an alley behind Smitty's bar. But, overall, Country Corners was a quiet, off-the-beaten-path kind of town.

Liz hit her transmit key. "Dispatch, give Darlene a call. I know it's her day off but I want all hands on deck. Send the rest of the team to the site. And don't forget to notify Matt."

"Team already dispatched, Sheriff, as well as the coroner. Sal handled it. He called Darlene in, too."

"Good. En route in five."

Code 187. Location 145 Creek Trail.

Liz knew this address. She knew these people. Kate Henderson sang in her church choir. Her husband, Dave, had done work for her at the station. Sliding behind the wheel of her patrol car, she washed a hand over her face and offered up a silent prayer.

Dear Lord, please be with me this day. Guide me. Strengthen me. Give me the wisdom and courage to face what lies ahead.

She was ready—or as ready as she ever would be. With a sigh and a heavy heart, she turned the key, felt the powerful engine surge to life and pulled away from the curb.

Liz passed the post office, Ms. Willowby's general store, the pharmacy and Clancy's hardware store as she drove through the center of town. People bustled up and down the street—business as usual.

How could this be happening here?

Almost everybody knew everybody. The town was like one big family—dysfunctional at times, sure—but still a family.

Liz chewed on her bottom lip. That's what was bothering her the most. She couldn't wrap her mind around the idea that one of their own might have been responsible for three murders.

She looked at her whitened knuckles and loosened her death grip on the steering wheel. As she reached the outskirts of town and drove into more rural territory, she tried to remember the conversation she'd had with Kate after church on Sunday. Kate had seemed preoccupied and Liz had asked if everything was all right. Kate said they had a big decision to make and asked Liz to say a prayer that they would make the right one. Now Kate's address was a murder scene.

The patrol car bucked and bumped as Liz turned off the highway and onto the dirt road leading to the Henderson house. She hugged the right side of the narrow road to let the coroner's van pass on its way back to town and breathed a sigh of relief. She wouldn't be human if she didn't admit she was grateful she was arriving here after the bodies had been removed.

Liz made a sharp right and drove down the graduated bend of the graveled circular driveway. It was hard not to catch your breath when the two-story house came into view. The white-clapboard pillared colonial rested at the top of the curve like a sentinel keeping watch on comings and goings. The black shutters and the deep burgundy front door provided a sharp contrast to the stark white. The house and property spoke money. Not rich, upper-crust money. Liz could count on one hand how many people in Country Corners filled that bill. But comfortable money, the kind that said, *We're living the American dream.*

Look where that dream had gotten them.

She caught a glimpse of parked cars and bustling activity as she pulled her car to a stop.

"Sheriff."

Paul Baxter, her youngest deputy, called to her as she stepped from her vehicle. His slim build and fair complexion reminded her of her brother, Luke. Maybe that's why she carried a soft spot for him. His eyes darted back and forth between Liz and the house. His facial expression told her he'd rather be anywhere, even cleaning out sewers barefoot, than here. But she gave him credit. He was doing his best to remain calm and professional.

"Baxter." She strode past him, walking toward the house, and he fell in step behind.

"Matt carted the bodies to the morgue less than five minutes ago, ma'am."

"I know. I passed him on the road."

Paul caught up and matched his stride with hers. "We've cordoned off the crime scene."

More nervous, useless words since Liz could already see the yellow tape roping off the entire front porch. Pausing a second to take a good look at her deputy, she noted the pallor of his skin, the slight trembling of his fingers against his belt.

"Are you okay, Paul?"

When he looked at her, she was taken aback for a moment by the wetness glistening in his eyes.

"I've never seen anything like it, ma'am." He drew in a deep breath. "Who could do something like this?"

She placed a comforting hand on the young man's shoulder. "That's what we're going to find out, Paul. Now, why don't you head back to the office? The others can walk me through the crime scene. You start writing up your report and we'll talk later."

The deputy grabbed at that lifeline, turned and almost sprinted to his car. His reaction made Liz steel herself for what she was about to see.

"Hello, Tom." Liz ducked under the crime scene tape and greeted her most veteran officer, Tom Miller, near the front door. She looked at the ugly bruise on his cheek. "What happened to you?"

"Danny Trent had a few too many at Smitty's bar last night and took a swing at Ralph. I tried to stop it and my face got in the way."

Liz sighed. Danny Trent was becoming a regular customer at the jail these days. She'd had a couple of altercations with him herself. Even had to ticket him just last week for DUI. "Did you run him in?" Liz asked.

"Nah. Just booted his butt out the door. Told him to go home and sleep it off."

One look at the older man's bruised knuckles told Liz just how Tom had booted Danny out the door. She almost felt sorry for Danny...almost.

The older man tilted his head. "Where's Paul going?"

"He looked a little green around the edges. I sent him back to the office."

"You baby him too much. Your father would've kicked his butt around the block. How else you gonna make a man out of him?"

Her father, Arthur Bradford, the former sheriff for over thirty years, controlled his town with an iron glove resulting in minimal crime activity and making Country Corners an ideal place to raise a family. But as much as she'd loved her father, she also knew he had bullied anyone different, creative or fragile. Liz had witnessed one too many times how officers like Tom and her father had toughened boys up. She wanted no part of it on her watch. She ignored Tom, adjusted her sunglasses and turned her attention to Detective Sal Rizzo, her right hand…and best friend.

"What have we got?"

"We've got a slaughter, that's what we got." Tom spoke before Sal had a chance to answer. He lifted his hat and raked a hand through his gray hair. "I worked for your daddy for almost thirty years, Sheriff, and we ain't never seen the likes of this." He lowered his voice and whispered in a protective, almost fatherly way, "Are you gonna be all right? Nobody would fault you none if you decide not to do a walk-through on this one. I can tell you what you'd see inside and you can get the rest from pictures."

Ever since she'd stepped into her father's shoes as sheriff, she'd been trying to prove her own worth and not be seen as Bradford's kid. She knew her lithe figure, blond hair and blue eyes didn't paint a picture of a tough, mean, legal machine, but she could hold her own and then some.

Liz peered over the top of her sunglasses and stared at the man eyeball to eyeball. At times like these, she was grateful for her five-foot-eleven-inch height. "I'm going to accept those remarks as well-meaning concern, Deputy Miller, and not that you question my ability to do my job."

A flush rose on the officer's neck. "Course not, Sheriff. You're great at your job. Your daddy would be proud."

Liz sighed. She knew that was the best she was going to get out of Miller. He was from the old school. It was difficult for him to see women as cops and more difficult to have one as his boss—particularly one he'd tripped over for years as she crawled and romped under her daddy's feet.

Her radio crackled. "Bravo 24. Code 117—15 Briarcrest Road, Apartment seven."

Code 117. Domestic dispute.

Danny Trent must have woken up with a hangover and decided to wipe the floor with his wife, Cathleen—again. This was turning out to be a busy morning.

"Tom, call it in. Since you've already had one run-in with Danny, you can have the pleasure of handling this one. Sal and I will finish processing the crime scene here."

"Suits me. I saw enough of that mess in there to last me a lifetime." The older man shuffled away, speaking into his mike as he went.

Sal escorted Liz the few remaining steps to the house, filling her in on the way. "The place has been ransacked top to bottom. Every drawer opened. Things tossed and smashed. But as far as I can see, it wasn't a robbery."

"How can you be sure?"

"The television and surround-sound system are still standing there large as life in the living room. The lady's purse is lying on the kitchen floor with about fifty dollars' cash still in it. A nice-size diamond ring was still on Mrs. Henderson's left hand when we found her. Mr. Henderson's wallet with cash and all his charge cards are still inside, too. If the family interrupted a burglar and it went bad, he would have at least scooped up that stuff before he took off."

"Makes sense. Let's take a look."

Sal opened the front door and stood to the side.

Liz slipped her hair inside a net. She accepted the paper booties that Sal handed her and put them over her shoes. With the use of DNA results in court, combined with advances in forensic testing, it was more important than ever to keep a clean crime scene. She was thankful that when she'd been elected to office she'd put those procedures into play and her investigation team honored them, even if they did have to ship things to state labs because they couldn't afford their own equipment.

"Where's Darlene?"

"She's inside placing the evidence placards and taking pictures."

"Okay. Let's get this over with, shall we?" Then she stepped inside.

Liz didn't realize she'd been holding her breath until the ache in her chest reminded her that her lungs were about to explode. She coughed out the pent-up air and quickly inhaled, pulling in lifesaving oxygen, only to realize that it was tinted with the coppery scent of blood.

She paused for a moment in the foyer, so stunned by the chaos that she didn't know where to look first. She found it difficult to absorb the total destruction. What hadn't been tossed around looked like it had been shoved aside or turned over. Liz stepped to the bottom of the staircase and her eyes traced a path toward the top. She stared at the white chalk outline about halfway up.

"That's where we found Kate Henderson," Sal said. "Four gunshot wounds to the back."

Liz couldn't picture the singing-in-the-choir Kate with the outline sprawled on the stairs. A deep sadness came over her. She hadn't known the woman well but no one should die like this.

"Morning, Sheriff."

Liz turned toward the voice and saw Darlene standing by the kitchen. She held yellow placards in her gloved hands. Her pale complexion, framed by short carrot-colored curls, looked even paler than usual.

"I think it started in here." Her deputy gestured behind her.

When Liz reached the kitchen doorway, her eyes widened but she fought hard not to let any other sign of emotional distress cross her face. The dozens of yellow evidence placards looked out of place—almost like a field of spring flowers planted in a valley of destruction. The kitchen, a place for happy family gatherings, was now a gruesome crime scene depicting violence and loss. It was one she wished she hadn't had to witness and one she knew she wouldn't soon forget.

"Darlene and I talked about it, boss." Sal came up behind her. "Best we can figure, Mrs. Henderson came in the back door unexpectedly."

"Yeah," Darlene said, stress evident in her voice. "See…" She pointed to a woman's purse and bags of spilled groceries strewn by the back entrance. "We think she surprised her husband and his assailant while they were in the middle of a fight. She got scared and dropped everything."

"It looks like she tried to run past them. Almost made it, too." Sal pointed to the stain on the door frame. "But the killer must have grabbed her. Looks like she slipped and hit her head against the doorjamb. But it didn't knock her out."

Darlene picked up the conversation. "Mr. Henderson probably jumped this guy from behind and tried to pull him off his wife. We figure that's when she raced past them and headed up the stairs."

The three of them retraced their steps and returned to the foyer. Sal pointed a finger at the chalk outline. "She made it halfway up before she was shot."

They climbed the stairs and carefully skirted the chalk outline.

At the top of the stairs, there was a loft. At the end of a six-foot railing was a short hall that led to the bedrooms. The three of them stared down at the foyer below for a better view of the crime scene.

"This doesn't make sense." Sal's puzzled expression twisted his lips in a frown and left deep parallel creases across his forehead.

"When does murder make sense?" Liz asked. "But killers always have a reason that makes sense to them— even if it's illogical to us. Our job is to do our best to figure it out."

Liz swept the area again with her gaze and offered up a silent prayer.

Dear Lord, please help me bring the person who did this to justice.

"Still…" Sal looked at Liz. "You'd think she would have tried to run out the front door. Why was she running upstairs?"

"Maybe this might have something to do with it."

Darlene, standing in the hallway entrance, held up a large plastic bag filled with a white powdery substance. "I spotted the edge of this bag sticking out from between the box spring and the mattress in the master bedroom."

Sal took the bag and opened it to examine the contents. "Cocaine. Looks like we have our motive. Drug deal gone wrong."

Liz chewed on her lower lip. "The Hendersons? Drug

dealers? I don't know, Sal. It's hard to believe the Hendersons were involved with drugs."

"Just how well did you know these people, Sheriff?" Sal asked. "Didn't they just move here this year?"

"I didn't know them that well. I knew Kate from casual encounters at church. All of us have met Tom. He's done some computer work for us at the station."

"Isn't he the guy who installed the new software and GPS system in our patrol cars?" Darlene asked. "He updated the software on our desk computers, too. He didn't look like a druggie to me."

"You know what all druggies look like?" Sal mocked. "I've been wasting my time. I should drive you around town and let you point out the possible druggies who may have killed that dealer behind Smitty's bar last week."

"Knock it off, Sal. There's a time and place for teasing and this isn't it," Liz reprimanded.

Sal raised his hands in a gesture of surrender. "Just saying, boss. These days drugs are everywhere."

Liz sighed. Sal was right. Whether she liked the idea or not, drugs had crept into her quiet little community. But she also agreed with Darlene. It was difficult picturing the Hendersons as part of that seedy side of life.

Needing to get back to the station to begin organizing the investigation, Liz glanced at her watch and asked, "Who did you call to take Jeremy and how long ago did they leave?"

Sal and Darlene glanced at each other and then gave her a blank look.

"Don't know what you're talking about, Sheriff." Sal shot her a hard stare. "Who's Jeremy?"

A sense of dread raced up and down Liz's spine. "Jeremy is their five-year-old son."

"The Hendersons had a son?" Darlene asked.

"Yes. A special-needs child."

"I checked the house myself, Sheriff. There's nobody else here."

"He has to be, Sal. Kate homeschools him. They don't have any relatives living nearby that would be taking care of him." Liz pushed past Darlene frantically. She raced from one bedroom to the next, checking the closets, looking under the beds. She came up short in the doorway of the master bedroom and looked hurriedly around the room. Trying to keep the panic out of her voice, she called his name.

"Jeremy."

Silence.

Liz dropped to her knees beside the master bed and looked underneath. Nothing. She raced to the closets. Tom's closet was filled with shirts, pants, sneakers and polished shoes all organized and in their proper place—but no Jeremy.

Her eyes made a quick sweep of Kate's closet, skimming over the shoe racks and storage bins. Her hands brushed aside the dresses, blouses and slacks.

She raced to the bathroom and looked inside the shower stall, even opened the linen closet.

"Jeremy."

"I told you, boss," Sal called from the doorway. "There isn't any kid."

A sense of unease crept up her spine. She suddenly remembered something Kate had told her about Jeremy. He liked to burrow under things. She raced back to Kate's closet.

"Jeremy?"

Her eyes searched the contents on the floor. The storage bins. The pile of folded blankets in the back corner.

Then she froze.

* * *

Dr. Adam Morgan's tall, imposing presence and crisp stride made people move out of his way without the need to ask. He didn't pause at the nurses' station or pull a chart or even speak to anyone for directions. It wasn't necessary. He could see the police officer sitting on a chair outside the corner room at the end of the hospital corridor and he didn't waste any time getting there.

He flashed his identification badge and shifted his weight from one foot to the other while he waited for the officer to check his name against the list of people allowed access to the room. When he received the okay, he pushed open the door, strode into the room and then came to an abrupt stop.

Lizzie.

When he delivered his medical report to the sheriff's department later today, he fully expected her to ask him to come in and answer some questions. Knowing her first impression of him after all these years would be important to what he hoped to achieve now that he'd moved back, he'd been trying to brace himself for it, trying to prepare how he'd act, what he'd say. But he hadn't expected the encounter to be this soon.

Not here, sleeping in a chair beside the hospital bed with her arm outstretched protectively over the sedated child.

Not now.

His heart skipped.

Her features were exquisite—smooth skin, gently sloping nose, cheeks rosy with sleep. Her teenage lankiness had blossomed into softly rounded, female curves. The golden highlights in the loose bun tucked behind her neck caught the sunlight from the window. She was even more beautiful than he remembered.

He didn't think he had made a sound but her eyes shot open.

The electric shock of sky blue looking back at him pierced his heart and froze him in place. A slow, sleepy smile tugged at the corners of her mouth when she saw him. Happiness lit her eyes, basking him in sunshine. He had missed this so much over the years—and then she came fully awake. The smile faded. The brightness dimmed. Being a psychiatrist, Adam recognized the flash of pain and hurt that danced across her features before she masked her emotions with another one—anger.

"Adam." He tried not to wince at the cold tone in her voice.

"Good morning, Lizzie."

He knew it would be difficult seeing her again, but even years of studying human behavior hadn't prepared him for the waves of shame and pain that engulfed him. After what had happened to her brother, Luke, Adam had believed he was doing what was best for Lizzie when he left. At the time, he'd convinced himself that he'd be the only one who would be hurt.

It took just a glance at her face to make him realize just how wrong he had been—about everything. He'd abandoned her when she'd needed him most. He had made a huge mistake and compounded it with more wrong choices. He'd failed her. After all these years, there was probably nothing he could do to fix it.

But he was going to do his best to try.

"Good morning." The soft, wistful sadness in her tone made him feel as if someone had reached inside his chest and squeezed his heart. "I heard you were back in town."

"I didn't expect to see you this morning."

She smiled sadly and shrugged. "Why would you?"

It was the words *not spoken* that filled the room and heightened the tension between them. The mild censure in her last question was understandably deserved. He'd left without a word and he had returned—still, without a word.

She stood up, stretching her arms and back like a cat after a summer nap, and stepped forward. "I suppose we should talk." She nodded toward the tiny body covered with white sheets lying on the bed. "About Jeremy."

"How long have you been here?" He moved toward the bed to check his patient's monitors.

"All night."

That surprised him and he turned to look at her. "Why? Doesn't he have any family? Grandparents?"

"No. Kate told me that Dave lost his family in a car accident when he was a teen. Her father died of a heart attack a couple years back. Her mother's alive but has dementia and is living in a nursing home in Poplar Bluff."

"Aunts? Uncles?"

"My team will check it out but I don't think so."

"Poor little guy. As if autism wasn't a big enough challenge for him." He brushed his hand over the sleeping boy's head and then turned his attention back to Liz.

"So, why did you stay? You have a guard right outside the door."

"He's afraid of uniforms."

"What?"

"Jeremy." She stretched again and rubbed her lower back as though trying to work out a kink. "Kate…that's his mother…*was* his mother…" She bit her lower lip, frowned and looked across the bed at him. "Anyway, she told me once that Jeremy is terrified of people in uniforms. I thought the sight of the medical and police uniforms might send him over the top. I've met Jeremy a couple of times when Kate brought him with her to church. He might remember me. I thought I should stay close by to see if I could help when he wakes up."

Adam gave her a closer look and noted for the first time the loose flowered blouse covering her uniform. Only the bottom of her holster peeked from beneath the edge. If the boy did wake up, what he'd see was a pretty lady and lots of flowers—not a cop.

A wave of respect washed over him. She'd grown up to be a caring, intelligent woman. But then, he'd always known she would because that's what she'd always been. Most teenagers are self-serving and selfish until they find their place in the world. Lizzie was an exception. She was always loving, kind, trusting. It was the trusting part that made another wave of guilt wash over him.

"I'm sorry I wasn't here when the boy arrived last night. I had an emergency in Poplar Bluff. But the hospital staff updated me by phone."

"That's okay. The staff sedated him almost immediately and he's been sleeping ever since." She gently brushed the boy's hair off his forehead and then raised her eyes to his. "I was surprised to hear that you've moved back to town."

"Why? This is my home."

"Really?" She tilted her head and studied him. "It didn't seem to stop you from leaving it the first chance you got."

Ouch. There it was. The elephant in the room.

He recognized the challenge behind her words. She had a chip on her shoulder and she was daring him to address the issue or try to knock it off. He knew anything he said right now would open old wounds and change nothing, so he remained silent.

"I'm sorry," Liz said. "That was mean." She chewed on her bottom lip, something he remembered her doing when she was nervous or upset.

"Forget it." He smiled at her and hurried to change the subject. "Right now, I'm filling a temporary consultant position in Poplar Bluff. It's not that long a drive from here. They had a real need and I owed a friend a favor. But as soon as they hire a replacement, all my attention will be here. I have big plans for Country Corners."

Liz grinned. "Really? You sound pretty excited. What kind of plans?"

For an instant, it felt like old times again.

When they were in high school, Liz had always been willing to listen and often offered sage advice beyond her years when he needed it. He thought he'd burst with his need to tell her about his plans for the community. His plans included her. He'd done his research before returning. He knew she was still single and not seeing anyone special. He was here to make amends, to right wrongs, to win her back.

One look into her steely, challenging gaze told him it was going to be more like *Mission: Impossible* than the uphill battle he had expected. But he was going to try.

"I'd like to tell you all about it. Maybe over coffee?" He hoped she'd still be able to read him, to sense his sincerity, at least.

Indecision and wariness flashed across her face. She opened her mouth to respond but he spoke first.

"But this isn't a good time. Give me a rain check?"

She closed her mouth and just stared at him.

He nodded at the tiny body lying on the bed. "Right now, I'm only interested in what you can tell me about this boy."

When she looked across the bed at him, there was a telltale glistening in her eyes. He wasn't sure if it was his words or the child's situation that caused her such pain. His gut twisted when he realized it was probably both.

"This little boy has lost everything and everyone," Liz said. "He's so young and vulnerable and…"

"Autistic?"

"Yes, autistic. Kate told me that he was making great progress with his verbal skills. And even though he still wasn't a fan of eye contact or light touch, he would crawl into her lap and allow her to hug him or sit quietly while she rocked him."

She blinked several times and her eyes hardened. "I need to get the guy who did this. I'm *going* to get this guy no matter what."

Adam nodded his understanding and empathized with her. A person capable of destroying a family as though they were without value or worth did not belong on the streets.

"Was the boy a witness?" Adam asked.

"I don't know. I think so, but I'm not sure. We found him hiding in the back of his mother's closet beneath some folded blankets and clutching his teddy bear. His hair was plastered to his head with sweat and his clothes…" She took a deep breath. "His pajamas were splattered with…" She tried to shake the image out of her head and sighed heavily. "After we found him, we took a second hard look at the crime scene. Some of the smears could have been his footprints near his mother's body and, again, in the kitchen by his father."

Adam looked at the sleeping child and his heart constricted. It would be hard enough to help a small boy rid himself of the fear of monsters after the experience he'd had. An autistic boy would present a bigger challenge.

Anger simmered right beneath the surface. In his profession, no matter how often he'd come in contact with the face of evil, it still never ceased to surprise him. "Did he say anything when you found him?"

Liz shook her head. "Sal and I found him. He took one look at our uniforms and got hysterical. Remembering what Kate had told me about uniforms, I slipped on one of his mother's blouses. I told Sal to call the paramedics and to go into Dave Henderson's closet and find shirts, hopefully large enough, for everyone to wear until we could get the child calmed down.

"But Jeremy continued to scream and thrash about so much I had to forcibly hold him down until the paramedics arrived so he wouldn't hurt himself. I wrapped my arms around him and held him against me as tightly as I could. After a few moments, it seemed to calm him"

Adam nodded. "You did the right thing. Many autistic children can't tolerate light touch but crave deep pressure. Just like we swaddle infants in blankets to provide them with a sense of security, sometimes autistic children experience sensory overload and need swaddling as well to help them calm themselves."

She washed a hand over her face and Adam realized just how exhausted she was.

He walked around the bed and stood beside her. He had to fight the urge to pull her into his arms and comfort her. But after what he'd done, the poor choices, the mistakes, he didn't deserve her friendship or her forgiveness—yet. But that wasn't going to stop him from trying. What he needed was time to prove he had changed and convince her that he was worth a second chance.

Instead, he placed a comforting hand on her shoulder. "You need to go home, Lizzie, and get some sleep.

Doctor's orders." He grinned, trying to lighten the somber mood.

"I can't. I have to get to the office. I'm sure the state boys have arrived by now. We have to form a task force and discuss investigation strategies."

"Call your office on the way home. Delegate tasks to other people." He clasped her forearms and gently pulled her up to face him. "I've heard you are a good sheriff, Lizzie Bradford. Rumor has it that you are a great sheriff. But an exhausted, dead-on-her-feet sheriff isn't going to get the job done. Go home. Grab a couple of hours' sleep. The state police will still be here when you wake up."

"You're right." She smiled at him and there it was again, that bolt of sunshine hitting him in the face. Her smiles had always had that effect on him. They looked into each other's eyes. Slowly, a tension, an awareness of past relationships, past hurts surfaced between them and he watched again as memories stole her smile away. She broke eye contact, glanced over her shoulder at the boy and said, "Please take good care of him, Dr. Morgan."

She crossed the room and paused in the doorway. "And Adam…" When she had his attention, she continued. "Call me Liz. You can even call me Sheriff. Nobody calls me Lizzie."

He arched an eyebrow. "That's all I ever called you."

"I know." Her words held a sadness that almost broke his heart. "But not anymore."

Then she slipped out of the room.

TWO

"Sal, can you come in here for a minute?" Liz placed her purse in the bottom drawer of her desk.

The wiry Italian strode in. His brown shoulder harness held his Glock in place. Muscular biceps puffed out the short sleeves of his black T-shirt. A thin gold necklace ringed his neck. He grinned, his teeth white and even, and it was all Liz could do not to laugh. He was a walking caricature of a mafioso wannabe— an Italian tough guy. He knew it and played it to the hilt for the ladies. She'd found herself immune to this particular part of his charm years ago.

Sal folded his wiry body onto one of the straight-back chairs in front of her desk and crossed an ankle on top of his knee.

"Never thought you'd be one of the missing-in-action's. Where you been? The spa?"

"I wish." Liz ignored his lighthearted teasing. He'd been her right hand for over four years now and she didn't know what she'd do without him. "Wait a minute. Does Country Corners even have a spa?"

"Sure does. I heard the Thompson pig farm offers mud baths at half price this week only and they're selling fast."

"That so?"

"Has to be true. I got it straight from Gertie Simpson's mud-caked lips."

Liz laughed out loud at the mental image of old maid Gertie Simpson covered with mud and thinking it was a beauty remedy.

"Okay, I admit that was a good one. Now, get serious and fill me in." Liz sat down and pulled her wheeled chair closer to her desk. "I take it you met with the state boys."

"Sure did. Detective Frank Davenport will be acting as liaison between our people and his men. They've agreed to handle the physical evidence—follow up with the state lab on the ballistic reports, prints and so on. They're also investigating the Hendersons' background prior to their move here."

Liz nodded and continued listening.

"Darlene enlarged all of the crime scene photos. She gave copies to Davenport and posted the other set to our board in the conference room."

Liz breathed a sigh of relief. Adam had been right. A couple hours of sleep hadn't prevented progress from being made on the case.

"Anything helpful in the photos?"

Sal shrugged and took a sip of coffee from the cup he'd carried in with him. "Not yet. You know how that goes. You don't know what is or isn't helpful until you have more of an idea about what happened in the first place."

"Thanks, Sal. I appreciate you coordinating things for me."

"No problem." He grinned at her like a kid who'd nabbed the top score on a school test and then continued updating her. "Our department's handling the investigation of the Hendersons since their move here in January. I'm running a check to see if there are any business ties we should be looking into. Paul's checking out Mrs. Henderson's social calendar. He's also interviewing neighbors to see if anybody saw anything—which is unlikely since the houses are so remote and secluded out there, but it's worth a shot. Miller's off this shift. I sent him home. I figure the guy's kissing retirement. Don't see any reason to ask him to work double shifts. Not yet, anyway."

"Darlene?"

"She's on a B and E call. I don't know—home invasions, murders, dead drug dealers, breaking and entering. All of a sudden our quiet little town isn't so quiet anymore."

"Tell me about it." Liz pulled a mug out of her top drawer and looked longingly at Sal's coffee cup.

He laughed. "Want me to grab you a cup of coffee, boss?"

"I'll get some in a minute. Want to catch up first."

He leaned over and poured half of the contents of his cup into hers. "Here, that should hold you over."

Liz grinned, leaned back in her chair and took a welcome sip of the hot liquid. "What would I do without you, Sal?"

"Just remember that when reviews roll around," Sal quipped.

"I'm glad you sent Tom home. We don't need two cops dead on their feet. I was at the hospital all night and had to grab a couple of z's myself. My mind was becoming mush."

"How's the kid?"

"They had to sedate him. He hasn't come out of it yet."

"I still can't believe there was a kid in the house and the killer missed him. I can't believe *we* missed him the first go-round."

"He hid in his mother's closet under a pile of blankets. Thank the good Lord, the killer did miss him," Liz replied. "He's such an adorable little boy...and he's our only witness."

"Think he'll be able to identify the shooter?"

Liz leaned back and gazed up at the white ceiling tiles. "I really don't know. He's only five. Besides, he's autistic."

"Autism. I've heard of it but don't know exactly what it is."

"It's a psychological disorder that affects language and socialization skills. Even if he saw the killer, I'm not sure he would be any help in identifying him."

"So, what you're telling me is that we have a witness that can't tell us what he witnessed. What kind of luck is that?"

"At least the little guy is alive. That's a plus. We'll know more when he wakes up."

"Do you want me to head over to the hospital and see if he's awake yet? I don't have a lot of experience with kids, but I'm willing to give it a try and see if I can get something helpful out of him."

"No, but thanks. Dr. Morgan is a highly respected psychiatrist. He's taking care of Jeremy. He'll let us know the second anything changes."

Sal slammed his foot back to the floor and stood up. "Then I'm out of here. I'm headed over to Henderson's business. Try to see if anyone there got passed over for a promotion or had their nose bent out of shape for any other reason."

"Be sure to report in," Liz called to his departing

back and laughed when he waved her away like the nag she sometimes knew she was.

The following morning, after several hours of fielding phone calls, reading reports and reviewing the crime scene photos, Liz came up for air. Progress on the case was slower than she'd like, but at least it was moving forward.

Liz glanced at the phone on her desk. Why hadn't Adam called? It had been three days since the murders and two since Adam took over Jeremy's case. There had to be some news to share by now.

The mental image of the six-foot blond-headed doctor played over and over in her mind.

Adam's back.

More handsome than ever in a mature adult way. The gangly teen finally grew into his feet, shoulders widened, muscles rock hard. He looked like that gorgeous young actor she'd seen when she'd watched an old classic movie marathon last weekend.

She hadn't known how she would feel when she saw him again. She expected to be disappointed, maybe even nurse a tinge of pain for old hurts—but instead she had felt an unexpected sadness for years lost. She'd expected to feel wells of hatred—but the Lord's Prayer had put a quick end to that.

What she hadn't expected was his ability to still snatch her breath away.

She thought she was going to melt into a puddle on the floor when he'd looked at her with those golden-brown eyes—and when he'd placed a hand on her shoulder to comfort her, she could have sworn her heart had physically flip-flopped in her chest.

She slammed her hand on the desk. What was the matter with her?

She'd decided years ago to pursue a career and not entangle herself with any permanent relationships.

It had been difficult following in her father's footsteps while trying to blaze a trail of her own. She'd had to devote herself one hundred per cent to her job. She'd worked hard, putting in long hours, but over the years it had paid off. She'd gained the respect of her team and her community. She couldn't afford to let down her guard now. She didn't have time for a man in her life, any man, and particularly one who had already broken her heart once before.

Another hour passed and Liz tried not to stare at the minute hand on the wall clock or jump each time the phone rang. Usually, she could lose herself in work, but not this time.

She drummed her fingers on her desk. What was she going to do with Jeremy when Adam did call and tell her the child could be released?

Darlene had done a thorough family background check on the Hendersons. Both Kate and Dave had been only children. No relatives to lay claim to the boy. So, what was going to happen to him?

Liz didn't have the heart to place him with Child Protective Services—not yet, anyway. Being autistic, she knew Jeremy would never understand what was happening to him. He'd been through so much already. He needed placement with a family trained to handle special-needs children and, unfortunately, she didn't think there would be much to choose from here in Country Corners.

Besides, Jeremy was a material witness for their murder case. Child Protective Services would have no means to protect him.

Liz stared out the window but didn't focus on anything she saw.

"What did you see, Jeremy?" Liz spoke the words aloud, almost as if the walls could talk and might provide the answers she desperately needed. She ran through the crime scene in her mind for what was probably the hundredth time.

If he had seen the killer, would he be able to identify the person from a photo lineup of suspects? If and when they ever came up with a suspect, that is.

She knew she had to try not to be so impatient. It had only been three days. They'd find something. They had to.

Liz stood up and looked through the blinds of her office window.

Great! Just what I need.

Two reporters from the local newspaper were buzzing about in the parking lot. How was she going to keep the situation under control if the national media picked up the story and ran with it? She could picture the sensationalized headlines.

Double Homicide in Small Town. Little Boy Only Survivor.

As soon as the press broadcast the existence of a sole survivor and possible witness, would the killer return to tie up loose ends?

A tight, painful knot formed in the pit of her stomach.

She glanced one more time at the clock. Jeremy had to be awake by now. Well, no more waiting. She grabbed her purse and muttered a string of unflattering descriptions of Dr. Adam Morgan for not calling her with an update. But why should he? Not calling her was his specialty.

* * *

Adam, standing in the hall in front of Jeremy's room, had an unobstructed view of Liz Bradford storming down the hall in his direction. If she could breathe fire and shoot lasers, he would be under attack at any moment. He knew he should keep a cool, calm, professional facade but he couldn't help himself. After all, this was Lizzie. When they were kids he had always gotten great pleasure out of pushing her buttons and watching her explode.

"It's about time you showed up," he said as soon as she was within earshot. "I was beginning to think you didn't care a hoot about this boy."

She came to such an abrupt halt it looked like she'd slammed into an invisible force field. Her eyes widened and her expression clearly showed she thought that he'd lost his mind. When she saw the grin on his face, she exploded right on cue.

"What are you talking about? I've been waiting to hear from you. Why haven't you called me with an update?"

Adam laughed out loud. "Calm down, Lizzie. I was just about to call you. I've been tied up with the boy."

His explanation seemed to appease her for the moment. When he took one step too close to her personal space, however, the warm fuzzies were gone and she stepped back.

She shifted beneath his gaze, and the sparks of anger he'd seen when she'd first approached quickly faded to something else—a wariness, almost like an animal that had been hurt and wasn't sure if it was going to be hurt again.

"I told you. Nobody calls me Lizzie."

"I do."

That's how he'd always think of her…Lizzie…tall, lanky, spirited, beautiful Lizzie. She looked up at him, and he thought he might drown in the pale blue of her eyes.

"Just tell me about Jeremy, please." Liz chewed on her bottom lip and waited for his answer.

"Okay…Sheriff." He nodded in deference to her request. "The boy is doing as well as can be expected under the circumstances. I was just about to call you. I need to know how much longer the house will be off-limits."

"Why?" She eyed him warily. "If you need clothes or toys or something, I would be happy to pick them up for you."

"That's not what I'm asking. I want to know if you've finished gathering evidence for the forensic portion of your investigation."

Liz studied him like a specimen under a microscope. "It's been three days. To my knowledge, we've already gathered all the forensic evidence. I'll have to check with Detective Davenport and verify that he's finished with the premises but the house will probably be available sometime tomorrow. Why?"

"Because I want to take Jeremy home."

"Home? To his home? You can't be serious." Her shocked expression was almost painful to see. "We haven't even had a team in there to clean the place!"

"I have already arranged for a cleaning service from Poplar Bluff that specializes in difficult stains and hazardous materials to go in and sanitize the house. They're on standby. As soon as you give me the go-ahead, I'll call them. The place will be spotless before we arrive."

She planted her hands on her hips. This time he could actually feel the heat from the laser look she shot him.

"The worst thing you can do is take him back into that house after everything that has happened. He's been traumatized. He doesn't need to be reminded of it."

"That's one school of thought." Adam kept his voice soft and calm so he didn't upset her more. "Some psychiatrists will tell you to avoid the place where a trauma occurred. I don't necessarily agree."

"Of course not," Liz hissed. "You're just like your father, aren't you? Following in the same footsteps like a clone instead of being your own person."

Adam felt a flush of anger warm his neck and cheeks at her biting barb. He realized he wasn't the only one who knew which buttons to push to get a rise.

"Don't do this, Adam. Please. You know what living in a place where a terrible tragedy occurred can do to the survivors. You saw the devastation up close and personal." The pleading tone in her voice verified his assumptions. This wasn't just about Jeremy. This was also about Luke.

"Jeremy has been through a major traumatic event. He needs to start to heal," he said.

"You think I don't know that?"

"Autistic children, on the whole, do not function well with sudden change. They require structure and repetition in their lives."

"Well, go ahead and provide him with structure and repetition—someplace else. You can't expect him to live in that house. Not now. Not since his family…"

Adam noted the near hysteria in her voice, the tense body language. Liz fought to remain calm and logical but she was losing the battle. The thought of returning Jeremy to the crime scene was obviously plunging her back in time…Luke and Jeremy…past and present… all swirling around in a painful mess and coloring her decisions. He knew he had to tread as lightly as possible but he also knew that he couldn't budge on this issue regardless.

"Liz, I understand your concerns. I do." He reached out a hand to comfort her. She moved away before he could connect and a shaft of pain hit his heart. He understood her desire to steer clear of him. He deserved it. He'd treated her abominably and he didn't deserve her kindness or forgiveness. But it hurt just the same.

He pulled his hand back, ran it through his hair and sighed heavily.

"I believe that being in familiar surroundings is the best thing for Jeremy. He is barely holding it together. I know he won't understand why his family isn't there, but their belongings will be…and his belongings…and I believe it will help him recover."

She continued to stare at him, her arms wrapped tightly and protectively around her body.

"Think about it, Liz. If he did witness the murder, it might trigger memories for him. You might find out something useful for your investigation." Adam caught her gaze with his. "Don't you want a professional with him when he begins to deal with his loss? I intend to be there with Jeremy. I will help him through it, I promise."

"You're moving into the house, too?"

"Yes, of course. Someone has to be with the boy until I feel we can safely transition him to a more permanent placement."

He could tell from the expression on her face that she was carefully weighing his words.

"Trust me."

Her eyes flashed at his words. "Trust you? Like my family trusted your father with my brother, Luke? Like I trusted you before…before…"

If she had slapped him with every ounce of strength in her body, it couldn't have hurt more. He knew she wasn't trying to hurt him. She was reacting to her own pain and not thinking. The words probably popped out of her mouth before she even knew what she was going to say.

But words can be as lethal as weapons and once spoken can't be erased.

Adam put up his own protective shield. He hardened his body language and the tone of his voice.

"Sheriff, it is my professional opinion that Jeremy Henderson needs to be in familiar surroundings in order to be able to process through his trauma. It will also give state officials time to work on a more permanent living situation for him, with people trained in dealing with his special needs. I am hoping not to get any opposition from the sheriff's department on this move. However, I am perfectly willing to get a court order if you insist."

"I think you are making a terrible mistake, Adam." Her eyes pleaded for understanding.

"Jeremy isn't Luke."

"You think I don't know that? The situation is totally different."

"That's right, Liz, it is." He waited, giving her the time she needed to think things through and come to grips with the situation.

She searched his eyes for some sort of reassurance. "You're moving into the house with him? You promise that he will never have to go through anything alone."

"Yes."

"Fine. Let me make a call. If Davenport is finished, you can have the cleaning crew go into the house today." She took a step toward him, her body taut, her posture threatening. "I don't want there to be anything, not one tiny thing, left behind to remind that child of the violence that happened in that house."

"Consider it done."

Adam could read her expression like an open book. She was struggling with the question of whether or not she could trust him.

They stood in the hospital hallway simply staring at each other. The minutes ticked away while her heart battled with her head. He knew from the steely glint in her eyes when she'd reached her decision—and somehow he didn't think he was going to like it.

"I'll meet you tomorrow at 4:00 p.m."

"That's not necessary, Liz. I can drive the boy myself."

"If you don't want to be forced into court for a ruling on this, then you'll do things my way." Her body language told him that her terms were nonnegotiable. "I am going to make sure nothing happens to that boy physically or emotionally. I will not let you repeat the damage your father did to Luke or to my family. I will be driving you to the house. Is that understood?"

Adam stifled the desire to lash back in anger and simply nodded his agreement to her terms.

Liz started to walk away and then turned. "By the way, if you are moving into the house with the boy, then be prepared, Freud, because I am, too."

He turned off his headlights, eased into a parking spot across the street from the hospital and cut the engine. He glanced at his wristwatch in the glow from the streetlamp. Ten minutes past midnight. He looked up and down the deserted street. No one around. He was safe for the moment.

He shouldn't be here. He knew that. But he couldn't stay away.

He stared into the darkness and wondered which lit window in the multifloored hospital belonged to the boy.

How could this happen? How could there have been a child in the house and he hadn't known? He hadn't seen any toys. There'd been a room filled with odd things like a funny-looking hammock swing hanging from the ceiling, some mats on the floor and a computer in the corner. He'd thought it was some kind of weird exercise room. It never dawned on him that there might be a kid in the house.

Passing headlights illuminated the inside of his vehicle. He ducked down and his heart surged with a rush of adrenaline. The risk he might get caught was like a natural high. Who needed drugs?

He did. Too often and too many.

He cursed himself for his stupidity. He shouldn't be in this situation. He should have taken care of everything at once.

Why hadn't he seen the kid?

He slammed his hand on the steering wheel.

Then a glimmer of hope filled his mind. If he hadn't seen the kid, maybe the kid hadn't seen him, either.

It was all over the news that there was something wrong with the kid. He had problems talking or something. So he probably couldn't tell anyone about him, anyway.

But could he afford to take the chance?

No.

He had no choice. He had to find out what that boy had seen before the boy had a chance to tell anyone else.

THREE

"You can stare at them photos till the cows come home and you're not gonna see anything you ain't seen before."

Liz startled at the sound of Tom Miller's voice but tried not to show it as she turned to face her deputy. She'd been standing in front of the white erase board, examining every inch of the crime scene photos.

"There has to be something here," Liz said. "Something that can steer our investigation in the right direction. What are we missing?"

"Wish I knew. Those pictures are making me plumb cross-eyed." Deputy Miller handed her a foam cup filled to the rim. The rich, robust aroma, unlike the mudlike brew they normally had available, woke up her senses. When he passed her a Boston cream doughnut, too, she almost drooled.

"You know me too well, Tom." She smiled, bit into the doughnut and licked the oozing, sweet cream off her lower lip. "This is just what I needed," she mumbled with her mouth full.

"There's a couple dozen more on the table in the break room. And a decent pot of coffee for a change.

Thought the men could use the boost before our meeting this morning."

He stood beside her and stared at the board. "I couldn't sleep last night so I came in early. I stared at the board for hours just like you been doing. Not one of them pictures talked to me. Leastwise, nothing I wanted to hear."

He shook his head and raised his hat brim then let it settle back down. "Thank God your daddy isn't alive. It would break his heart to see a family destroyed like this in his town." He glanced at her and a red flush crept up his neck. "No offense, Sheriff. I'm not sayin' that you're not just as torn up about all this."

"I understand, Tom. I miss him, too." Liz placed a comforting hand on his shoulder. "Don't worry. We'll get this guy."

Voices sounded behind them as the investigation team filed into the briefing room and took their seats around the conference table. Liz glanced at their brimming coffee cups and the doughnuts in their hands. She chastised herself for not thinking of it herself but was grateful that Tom had. She took a seat at the head of the table. Detective Davenport sat to her right. Sal pulled up a chair on her left. The rest of the men filled in the remaining seats.

"Good morning, gentlemen." She smiled at the men as they returned her greeting. "While you finish your breakfast, I'll get this meeting started so we can get back out there as quickly as possible."

She shuffled through some papers in the pile in front of her and pulled out a sheet of paper. "Darlene is off this shift. I have a copy of her preliminary report. The autopsy reports aren't available yet but we hope to have them by tomorrow. Detective Davenport's team has verified that the plastic bag we recovered from the Hendersons' bedroom did contain five pounds of high-grade cocaine."

"Five pounds?" Paul asked. "That's not recreational use. The guy was a dealer."

"Did they get any prints off the bag?" Tom asked.

"No prints. Not even Henderson's. It was wiped clean."

Sal looked puzzled. "That doesn't sit right with me. No prints? Not even his own? Why would the guy wipe his prints off the bag before hiding it under his mattress? Did he have some kind of sixth sense that he was going to get raided or something?"

"Maybe he wore gloves," Paul replied.

"Maybe," Sal answered. "But if he wore gloves every time he handled the bag, then where are the gloves? We haven't found any, have we?"

Liz scoured her evidence inventory sheets. "No gloves."

"See." Sal leaned back in his chair. "Something stinks and I can't quite put my finger on it."

"Moving on." Detective Davenport took over the lead. "Nothing significant has shown up in the Hendersons' background check. Henderson was a model employee and well liked at his old job. They hated to see him leave but were happy for him when they heard he planned to start his own computer tech firm."

"Anyone express any animosity about the move?" Tom asked. "Any signs of jealousy that the guy was going to run his own business?"

"Nothing that turned up in our initial interviews. Everyone seemed to sincerely wish him well. His boss not only gave him a letter of recommendation but was instrumental in helping him get his first client. Seems

Third National Bank has a branch in Country Corners and was updating their computer software. Since his old firm holds the account, the boss threw the local business his way."

"What about the boy's school?" Paul asked. "Anyone talk to any of his teachers? Maybe the parents had a falling-out with another parent or something."

"One of my men checked that out," Davenport replied. "Jeremy had been in an Easter Seals special education preschool class when they lived in Tennessee. Kate chose to homeschool him once they moved here but not because of difficulties with the schools or parents. She just wanted to take a more hands-on approach to his education. She continued to take him to Poplar Bluff for occupational therapy three times a week."

"Anyone know what brought them here in the first place?" Sal asked.

"I can answer that one," Liz said. "Kate told me that she was born and raised in Poplar Bluff, which has grown quite a bit since she was a kid. They talked about it and wanted to settle somewhere a little more rural. They thought Country Corners would be the ideal suburban setting to raise children and yet still be close enough to take advantage of the things more populated areas had to offer.

"Kate's mother has dementia and lives in a nursing home in Poplar Bluff. Our town is still close enough that she could take Jeremy for his therapy and visit her mom, too. Seemed like the ideal situation."

"Didn't work out quite the way they planned, did it?" quipped one of Davenport's men, who was immediately censured with a glare from his superior.

"How about you, Sal? Got any leads?" Liz asked.

"On the surface, it's a lovefest at this job, too. Everyone singing the boss's praises. But we all know that nobody likes to speak ill of the dead. I did a little digging and I found out that Henderson fired a couple of people this past year. Don't think they'll be singing his praises when I interview them."

Liz and Davenport absorbed the information and both nodded.

Brian Walker, one of the men on Davenport's team, spoke up. "I read in this morning's paper that the Henderson boy is being released today."

Liz winced. She wished there was some legal way to muzzle the press. How was she supposed to run an investigation when every move was broadcast to the public? Didn't the press know that killers read, too?

"Is that true?" Davenport asked. "Has anyone even talked to the boy yet? Does he know anything pertinent to our investigation?"

Liz spoke with authority. "Yes, it's true that Jeremy is being released this afternoon. So far he has not been able to respond to any questions regarding the murders."

"Released? Where? To whom?" Sal's expression looked annoyed that she hadn't shared this information with him earlier.

"Dr. Morgan is accompanying the boy to his home until we can make other arrangements."

Liz sighed deeply and leaned back in her chair, steeling herself to deliver the rest of her news.

"We can't ascertain yet if Jeremy witnessed the murder or not. But one thing we do know. That child saw his family lying dead. My goal is to bring the killer to justice and to help Jeremy feel safe again."

"Are you sure he saw what happened?"

Liz answered Tom's question. "The boy hasn't spoken a word about the incident so we're not sure yet what he witnessed, if anything at all."

"If he did witness his family's murder, how do you plan to keep him safe?" Sal asked. "I mean, once the killer reads the papers or hears on the news that he's been released, what's going to stop him from making a second run at the boy?"

"We are," Liz answered, putting a don't-dare-question-me tone in her voice. "I will be arranging for 24-7 police protection."

A low murmur traveled around the table.

Liz held up her hand for silence. "I know. Everyone's been working double shifts as it is. We are a small department with a small staff. I understand."

She glanced around the table. "I have a plan. Most of the coverage has already been arranged." Liz turned her attention to Davenport. "My team and I will be able to cover most of the time slots. I'll need to utilize your men on the graveyard shift so I can get some sleep. Can I count on you, Sergeant?"

"I'll make it happen."

"Thanks." Liz took a breath and prepared herself for dropping her next bombshell. "Dr. Morgan and I will be moving into the residence with the child."

Paul, who had been sipping coffee and eating doughnuts through the entire meeting, looked up. "You're moving in, Sheriff? What does that mean?" Still looking a little sick, even five days after the incident, her youngest deputy scratched his head and looked puzzled. "Are you just sleeping over there or what?"

"I'll be moving my office to the house. With computers, visual teleconferences and cell phones, I feel confident I can temporarily run my office from there. When there is an occasion that requires my presence outside of the home, I will arrange for one of our team or one of the troopers to stand in for me until I return. Our goal is to provide 24-7 protection for Jeremy and to catch this killer as quickly as humanly possible."

"And just how long do you think you're going to be able to run a sheriff's office from the house?" Sal's disapproval at this turn of events was evident in the sharp tone of his voice. "It's going to be hard enough protecting the boy. Aren't you making a target of yourself, too?"

"I will be protecting Jeremy." She looked directly at Sal. "And I appreciate your concern, Sal, but I'm a cop not the victim. I don't need protection."

Sal scowled, the news still not sitting well with him. "Do I need to remind you that the Henderson case isn't our only case?"

"I don't need to be reminded of my obligations—by you or anyone else." A tense silence descended upon the room. "That brings up another point. How is the investigation progressing with the drug dealer's murder? Any leads?"

Sal shrugged. "Nothing definite. Got a couple of nibbles I'm following up. I'll let you know if I turn up anything solid."

Liz nodded. "Have any of you been able to tie the cocaine in Henderson's possession to any of our known local dealers?"

"Still working on it. Nothing yet." Paul wiped the last of doughnut cream from his lip.

"What's on your agenda today, Tom?" Not willing to continue a verbal battle with Sal, Liz tried to steer the conversation in a different direction.

"Well, I love Country Corners same as the next fella," Tom said. "But all small towns, even ours, have secrets.

Maybe Henderson stumbled across one of those secrets and it got him killed. So, I'm gonna force myself to have tea with some of the old lady gossips in this town. Ain't no tellin' what I might find out."

Laughter rippled through the room.

"Good idea," Liz said.

"Well, then the way I see it," Tom said. "If we want this killer caught and our sheriff back in her office, then we better get off our butts and make it happen."

He spread a line of cocaine on the kitchen counter, twisted a dollar bill and snorted it into each nostril. The instantaneous rush raced along his nerve endings, filling him with an almost inhuman energy considering he'd had very little sleep since "the incident."

That's how he thought of it—the unfortunate incident. He hadn't planned it. He hadn't wanted it to turn out that way. He had just wanted to talk to the man, but things had gotten way out of control

He bounced on the balls of his feet and paced back and forth to the rap music on his radio with a nervous, uncontrolled energy. How did people listen to this crap? But he had to admit the rhythm sounded pretty good when you were high on coke.

His thoughts skittered back to the Hendersons. He hadn't wanted to shoot them. He rubbed his knuckles into his eyes and bounced and paced faster.

No.

It wasn't his fault. The wife had gotten a good look at him. He'd had no choice. Self-preservation. Isn't that a human's strongest instinct? He'd done it quickly. She hadn't suffered. That had to count for something, didn't it?

The music, if that's what you wanted to call it, ended

and the sound of the newscaster's voice caught and held his attention. He listened intently. They were reporting that the kid was going home today.

Now what was he going to do about that kid?

Liz Bradford stood beside her patrol car, lifted her face and basked in the warmth of the afternoon sun. She breathed in the floral scent of the last blooms of summer. And just as she'd thought five days ago, everything appeared normal. But there was nothing normal about a little boy returning to the house where his parents had been murdered. Sadness weighed heavily on her shoulders.

Liz adjusted her dark sunglasses and looked inside the glass doors to the hospital elevator bank. She hadn't waited long when Adam Morgan stepped off an elevator, leading Jeremy by the hand, and headed her way.

She'd felt guilty when she'd done it, but she had looked Adam up on the internet to see what he'd been up to over the years.… She'd been surprised to discover he'd won several awards for his work with children.

But, then again, Adam Morgan had been a bundle of surprises from the moment he'd returned. Not that it mattered. Liz had no time in her life for relationships, especially ones that had already failed so spectacularly. Her work was her life and she intended to keep it that way.

When they reached the car, the boy wrenched his hand out of Adam's, froze in place and flapped both of his hands in the air. "Stranger's car. Jeremy can't go. Stranger's car. Stranger's car."

Adam crouched down so he could be eye level with the child.

"Look at me, Jeremy."

"Can't go. Stranger's car."

Adam waited a second or two and then grasped Jeremy's chin. He turned the child's face toward him, released his hold and pointed to his own face. "Look at me."

Jeremy did as he was told.

"This is Sheriff Bradford's car. You remember Sheriff Bradford, don't you?"

Liz waved at the child, even though neither of them bothered to look in her direction.

"Sheriff Bradford is not a stranger. She is a friend and she is going to drive us home."

"Home. Jeremy wants to go home."

"Good." Adam straightened and gestured to the backseat. "Get in and we'll go home."

"Jeremy can't go. No. No. Stranger's car."

Adam lifted the boy and placed him in the protective child seat that Liz had already secured in the back.

Instantly, a high-decibel wail pierced the air. Jeremy flailed his arms and arched his body in a futile attempt to buck his body out of the car seat.

One of the nurses had followed them off the elevator and now handed Adam a small object that looked like a miniature Kevlar vest.

"What's that?" Liz leaned in so she could get a closer look.

"A weighted vest." Within seconds, he had the vest on the child and the car seat belted safely. Without a word, he walked around to the other side of the car and slid into the backseat beside the child.

"Thanks, Cindy." Adam reached through the open door and handed her a set of keys. "Tell Charlie to give us a couple of hours before bringing Rerun and the rest of my things over to the house. I want the boy to have some time to get acclimated to being home."

"Sure thing, Doc." Cindy flashed him a bright smile and the cutest little wave and then walked back inside.

Liz chewed her lower lip and tried not to grin.

Even in high school, Adam had never liked flirts and she could see the years hadn't changed him. She recognized the red flush on his neck, the sheepish look in his eyes when he looked up at Liz to see if she had realized Cindy was flirting with him. His discomfort was so genuine, so sweet, she almost laughed out loud. Almost. The child's loud, shrill screams made it impossible to focus on much else than saving her eardrums at the moment.

She climbed into the driver's seat and twisted her face toward the back.

"Why the vest?" She had to shout to be heard over the boy's screaming.

"Remember our conversation about swaddling? The weight of the vest and the snug seat belt should help Adam feel a little more secure on the trip home."

As if on cue, the boy continued to sob but the sounds no longer rent the air.

"Who's Rerun and Charlie?"

"I'll explain later. Just get us out of here."

A tap on the driver's side window drew Liz's attention. A woman she didn't recognize held a microphone in her hand. A photographer stood behind her with camera ready and probably rolling.

"Sheriff, is it true that you're taking the boy back to the scene of the crime?"

"Sheriff." A second voice grabbed her attention. Harriet Townsend, a reporter from the local paper, tapped on the passenger window. "Has the boy said anything to you yet? Is he able to describe the killer?"

Within seconds, Liz saw at least a dozen more people running toward the car. Heaven help them, their little hometown secret had leaked out and was now national news.

As reporters stormed the car and banged on the windows, Jeremy's cries began to intensify.

"Get us out of here before those idiots make the situation worse."

Liz ordered the people to step back and slowly eased her car through the growing crowd.

She heard Adam trying to soothe the screaming child. He spoke in short, concise sentences. His voice remained low and calm.

Liz pulled out of the hospital lot and moved into the flow of traffic. She glanced in the rearview mirror. Adam held a small wad of brightly colored putty in the palm of his hand. He squeezed and stretched the putty and then handed it to the boy and encouraged him to do the same. Sobs subsided into whimpers and then hiccups rather than tears.

Liz breathed a sigh of relief and turned her attention back to the road. She admired the way Adam was able to take charge of the situation and soothe the boy. Of course, he should know how. This was his job.

But not all psychiatrists knew what they were doing.

Fleeting thoughts of Luke surfaced and left a bitter taste in her throat.

She glanced in the mirror one more time. Satisfied with the peace that had descended upon the backseat, Liz allowed herself to relax. On the very slim chance that Dr. Adam Morgan was half as good as the reputation that preceded him, she conceded that maybe he was right. Maybe the familiar surroundings of his own home would be good for the boy. Maybe this wasn't going to be the full-blown disaster she'd anticipated after all.

But just in case, she started to pray.

He positioned himself on the ground, well hidden from view in the brush at the edge of the woods. He'd just surveyed the area with his binoculars for the fourth time in the past hour and was certain he'd picked the optimal spot. There were no houses, no hiking trails, no reason for anyone to be walking in this area. No witnesses.

He propped himself up on his elbows and raised the rifle to his shoulder. He adjusted the scope and aimed the weapon exactly at the crest of the curve in the road. He calculated wind velocity, car speed and made all necessary adjustments. He was ready.

Where were they?

Rivulets of perspiration dotted his forehead and slid down the back of his neck. Gnats buzzed around his head, and he steeled himself not to lose concentration and swat at them.

The news on the radio had prompted him to action. He'd raced to the Henderson house to make sure they hadn't arrived before him only to find hordes of media camped in the driveway looking for their lead story for the night.

Well, be patient, folks. Real soon now, I'm going to make sure you get the story of a lifetime.

He sniffed and wiped his runny nose on his sleeve. Hours ago, he'd shot up with heroin and cocaine, known on the street as speedballing. He needed another fix and he hated himself for it. The hit of cocaine he'd had in his kitchen wasn't taking the edge off the urge for more heroin. It simply energized him for this task so he wouldn't nod out.

When had he become a junkie? Nothing good came from drugs. He knew that. But still... How could he ever explain how great it felt to shoot up? The feel of the rush. Wired up. Energized. Alive. And then the nodding out. The deep well of black nothingness. Maybe it wasn't all bad.

He tapped his finger against the gun stock and tried to distract himself by beating out a rhythm to one of his favorite songs. A bead of sweat dripped into his eye and he cursed as he wiped it away. Boy, he needed another fix.

He shifted his weight and visually checked out his rifle. The barrel rested in the tripod. He adjusted the vertical cheek piece. He looked into the telescopic sight and then he saw them, approaching fast from the east. He eased his finger against the trigger and waited.

Any second now.

Wait for it.

Wait.

The police cruiser pulled into the curve.

FOUR

Liz glanced in her rearview mirror. Jeremy had drifted off to sleep clutching the teddy bear she'd brought to the hospital the night of the murders. His thumb barely clung to his lower lip. His short brown hair, drenched with sweat from his earlier temper tantrum, was plastered in little ringlets across his forehead. He looked so tiny…and innocent…and precious.

Her heart swelled with maternal instincts she hadn't known she had. Having children had never entered her mind, certainly not in the years she'd worked to achieve her status as sheriff of Country Corners. She hit the transmit key on her radio and reported her ETA to the dispatcher.

The air rent with a crack followed by another. Before she could identify the sound, the vehicle shuddered violently and the steering wheel jumped out of her hands.

It took a second for her to react.

But a second was all it took to career the patrol car out of control.

Liz grasped the wheel hard like it was the reins of a runaway horse. She tried to regain control but, traveling at more than fifty miles per hour, it was a lost cause. The car propelled toward the edge of an embankment. She knew if she continued in the direction of her skid, they would catapult into the air at the curve. She turned the wheel hard to the left, trying to compensate and grab hold of the road through the turn. The rear end continued to fishtail. At any other stretch of road, she might have been able to straighten out and regain control but not on this curve. It was just too sharp.

As the car went airborne, all Liz could do was yell, "Hold on!"

The road disappeared beneath her. Nothing but blue sky above and empty air surrounded them. Then the nose of the car dipped down, traveling at top speed back to earth. Seconds later the front grill hit the ground with a bone-jarring, crushing thud.

Upon impact, the air bags flew open and the force hit her chest and stole her breath away.

The car flipped upside down and continued to slide down the ravine on its roof, bumping...bucking... grinding over every stone, rut and pebble. The sound of tree branches scratching along the sides of the vehicle sounded like nails on a chalkboard.

Then absolute silence.

Liz didn't move. She couldn't. It took her a second or two to realize the crushing pressure on her chest was her seat belt holding her suspended in space and stealing whatever breath remained in her lungs.

Jeremy.

She pushed against the air bag and tried to find the release button on her seat belt.

"Jeremy."

Liz twisted her head to the side, throwing her voice toward the backseat. She stifled a scream.

Adam's face was mere inches from her own. He must have removed his seat belt so he could tend to Jeremy and had smashed against the wire barrier between the front and back seats. His eyes were closed and blood flowed down the left side of his face from a nasty-looking cut on his forehead.

"Adam!"

She couldn't move enough to see if he was still alive. She tried to turn her head far enough to see Jeremy. It was the deathly silence that frightened her. For once, she gladly would have opted for the sound of his ear-splitting screams.

Something heavy pressed against her lower body. She couldn't feel her legs. Panic washed over her. Why couldn't she move her legs?

She slid her arm up and reached the radio micro-phone.

"This is Bravo 24. Come in."

"This is Dispatch. Go ahead, Sheriff."

"Officer down. Vehicular accident. Send bus. Over."

"GPS location complete. Ambulance and backup en route."

Liz released the button and turned her face back toward Adam. She pushed the air bag away enough to get her hand free. Pain shot through her shoulder but she didn't stop. Once clear, she slid her fingers through the holes in the wire.

Please, God, let him be alive.

She poked the tips of her fingers through the mesh enough to feel his skin. It took several tries but she was finally able to press one of her fingertips against the carotid artery in his neck. His skin was warm and his pulse strong and steady. It was warm to the touch and Liz released a nervous laugh. He was alive.

Adam's eyes flickered open at about the same time a scared, protesting wail sounded from Jeremy.

Liz smiled wide and welcomed her tears of relief. *Thank You, Lord. We're alive.*

"Lizzie?"

"Adam. Thank God. How badly are you hurt?"

Adam raised his face off the wire mesh. His head spun and the hand he held against his face came away wet with blood. It took him a moment to get his bearings.

They must have been in an accident. But he couldn't remember any of it.

Adam ripped a piece of cloth from the tail of his shirt, and wrapped the makeshift bandanna tightly around his head to apply pressure.

"Are you okay? Adam, talk to me."

"I'm okay." He blinked his eyes and tried to clear his head. He stared unseeingly through the wire mesh and then his eyes widened as everything came into focus. "Liz! Are you hurt?"

She was crying…and grinning…and hanging upside down. *What had happened?*

"I'm okay, Adam. Check on Jeremy."

Immediately Adam turned his attention to the crying boy, who was also suspended from the ceiling. Expertly and slowly he moved his hands over the boy's body to check for any major injuries or breaks. When nothing seemed wrong, he released the seat belt and lowered Jeremy to a standing position in the tiny space in front of him.

Jeremy wrapped his arms around Adam and held on like he was never going to let go.

Adam twisted his left arm behind his back and pushed down on the handle, but the car door didn't open. Of course. The back doors in a police cruiser are automatically locked.

"Liz, are you hurt?"

"I don't think so."

"Can you open the back door?"

He heard her grunt and watched as she struggled to move.

"Can you get your seat belt unfastened and move yourself into an upright position?"

"I don't think so. The metal clasp on my seat belt is crushed. I can't release it."

"Are you sure you're not hurt?"

"I'm stuck. Something heavy is pinning my legs. But I'm not in any pain."

"Can you reach your radio and call for help?"

"I already did."

No sooner had she answered than the sound of multiple sirens filled the air.

She grunted and groaned and twisted. "Try it now."

"What?"

"The door."

Adam pressed down on the handle. He fell out. The short fall knocked the wind out of him. Jeremy tumbled with him, amazingly never letting loose of his death grip on him. He helped the boy to a sitting position.

"We're okay." Adam forced Jeremy's face around. "Look at me. I need to help Ms. Lizzie." He pried the boy's hands loose. "Sit here. Don't move. Do you hear me? Don't move."

Adam rushed around to the driver's side of the car. The entire front of the vehicle looked like a crushed tin can in a recycling bin.

Please, God, don't let Lizzie's legs be tangled in that mess.

Adam tugged on the door handle but it wouldn't budge. He shoved his fingers between the twisted door and the bent frame and then pulled with every ounce of strength in his body. Nothing.

"Try this. It's all I have for now." Darlene seemed to appear out of nowhere and Adam had never been happier to see anyone. He took the crowbar from her hand.

"I've radioed for the Jaws of Life unit. They should be here soon. Is the sheriff okay?"

"I'm fine," Liz yelled when she heard her deputy's voice. "Take care of Jeremy."

Darlene raced around the car. As she reached the child, she tripped over the teddy bear, which must have fallen out of the car when they'd exited. She sat on the ground, scooped the child up on her lap and handed him the stuffed toy.

Surprisingly, the boy's cries had stopped and he watched the commotion in silence, his thumb tucked in his mouth, his body gently rocking back and forth.

Adam glanced over at those serious brown eyes and worried that the boy might be going into shock. But there was nothing he could do for him right now. He hoped the paramedics would arrive soon. All he could think about at the moment was getting Lizzie out of this death trap.

He placed the crowbar in the opening again and pulled with all his strength. Still nothing. Not even the slightest budge. He pulled again and again.

Adam saw Sal slide down the ridge a foot or two, fall on his butt, and then regain his footing and continue his slide until he reached them. "Here's another crowbar. Maybe two of them will give us the leverage we need."

"Three are better than two." Tom Miller joined the two men.

Adam, Tom and Sal inserted the crowbars into the opening, used the force of their bodies as leverage and pushed down with all their might. On the second try they were able to pry the door open just wide enough that Sal could reach inside and cut Liz free of her seat belt. No longer bound, she was able to dislodge the computer console that had broken off and pinned her beneath the dashboard.

Once free, she slipped to the floor, which was actually the ceiling of her patrol car, and pulled her feet under her. Her face grimaced in pain and she tentatively ran a hand over her thigh. Her pant leg was torn and her hand came away wet.

The sight of red on her palm sprung Adam into action.

They needed to get Liz out of the car.

Now.

Before anyone else noticed the steady stream of gasoline slowly pooling around their feet.

"Can you climb out on your own?" Adam yelled.

"I don't think so. My leg doesn't seem to want to hold my weight."

"The door's not open enough to get you out," Sal yelled. "If we break the window, maybe we can hoist you through."

"Gas." Tom kept his voice low so only the other two men could hear. "We're standing in gasoline."

Adam locked eyes with the man. He kept his voice low and stern. "Then we better get your sheriff out of this car before it becomes her coffin. Right?"

The man squirmed beneath Adam's intense stare and then nodded.

Sal, with his slim, tall build, elbowed his way past Adam, flopped on the ground and shoved his arms inside the opening.

"Grab my hands, boss. We don't have any time to lose."

"Everybody hightail it to the road. Now!" Deputy Miller swung his hat back and forth as he ushered gathering onlookers up the embankment. As the smell of gasoline grew stronger, none of them needed a second invitation.

"That goes for you, too, Doc," Tom ordered.

"I'm not leaving Lizzie."

Tom grabbed Adam's arm and stepped between Adam and the car. "Sal's got it under control. Right now that boy up yonder needs you—and I'll be guessing the sheriff might need a little informal counseling, too, when all of this is over. Get going, Doc."

Adam fought the urge to push the older man out of his way. His adrenaline was pumping. He felt like a bull ready to charge anything and anyone in his path that tried to keep him from Liz. Until he saw her hands clasped tightly to Sal's wrists and knew the detective was going to get her out.

He locked eyes with Tom. The older man nodded and released his hold on Adam's arm. Reluctantly, Adam turned and climbed up the embankment.

From the top of the rise, Adam turned and watched Sal pull Liz into his arms. He could barely stand the feeling of failure that washed over him. It wasn't *his* hands that had pulled her from the wreckage. It wasn't *his* arms wrapped around her. He'd let her down—again. She'd been better off without him years ago and nothing had changed. She didn't need him now, either.

"Put me down." Liz wriggled and pushed against Sal's chest. "I can walk."

"We're almost at the top."

"Sal, I'm not kidding. Put me down. How do you

think it looks to all those people that the sheriff can't climb up this embankment under her own steam?"

Sal hesitated then let her slide to her feet, but he kept a steadying hand on her arm.

When they reached the crest of the hill, Liz nodded at Sal, mouthed the word *thanks* and then limped hurriedly straight toward the ambulance in search of Jeremy and Adam.

"Ma'am, better let me take a look at that leg. It might need stitches." A paramedic intercepted her before she'd reached her destination. He gestured to the gaping wound visible through her shredded pant leg.

"It's fine."

"It's not fine, ma'am. It's deep and nasty looking. Let me clean it up and pack it for you, at least until we can get you to a hospital."

"I said I'm fine. How are the boy and Dr. Morgan?" Liz looked beyond the paramedic's shoulder and saw Adam sitting on a gurney and another paramedic bandaging his forehead.

Jeremy was strangely quiet on the gurney beside him, particularly with all the uniforms milling about. But then she noticed that the boy was wrapped in the top of a scrub uniform. Adam must have requested an extra top from one of the paramedics. How creative for Adam to have eased Jeremy's fears by dressing the boy the same as the men around him.

Adam turned his head at the sound of her voice and looked out the back of the ambulance. He appeared defeated, guilty even. What did he have to feel guilty about? She'd been the one who had lost control of the car. Before she could draw close enough to speak with him, Sal grabbed her arm and spun her around.

"I told you this was a bad idea." Anger poured out of him like steam from a boiling teakettle.

"What are you talking about?"

"You should have put that kid in foster care, preferably in another county. We don't have the manpower to handle this."

"I lost control of the car. It has nothing to do with Jeremy."

"Really? How did you lose control?" He bounced on the pads of his feet, more agitated than she could remember ever seeing him. "Have you looked at that car? Someone shot out your tires! Think maybe that would make you lose control?"

"My tires?" Liz looked at the crumpled mass below. "Are you sure?"

"Of course I'm sure. Front and rear, driver's side."

"Leave her alone. Hasn't she been through enough?"

Liz sensed Adam's presence behind her. She could almost feel the brush of his breath on her neck. The temptation to turn and bury her face against his chest, feel the safe haven of his arms, was intense. But she didn't. She didn't need anyone's protection. She was the protector.

Sal stormed forward, forcing Liz to step aside. He poked Adam in the chest multiple times with his index finger. "This is your fault. Ever since you showed up, she hasn't used the brains she was born with. That kid belongs in the care of Child Protective Services. If you're so worried about him, then here's a suggestion for you. Why don't *you* take him some place far, far away? Neither one of you needs to be here mucking up this investigation and making it impossible for us to do our jobs."

"Sal, stop it." Liz stepped between the two men and

tried to keep her astonishment from showing on her face. "What's got into you? Stop it right now."

When Sal joined the force, they had flirted a bit with each other, tested the waters, so to speak. Once Liz realized Sal didn't share her faith, and probably never would, the relationship ended. They'd remained friends and over the years developed a tight, successful working partnership. Nothing more—at least on her part. "What were you thinking?" Sal got in her face. He continued to have trouble keeping his temper in check. "We're a staff of five. We can't protect you and the boy and work the case. Keeping him here is a death warrant. I could have been pulling your corpse out of that car."

One look at his flushed cheeks and overbright eyes turned Liz speechless. He still had feelings for her—and she'd never known.

"Hold on, son." Tom Miller stepped up and patted Sal on the back. "I know the tires were blown out but we don't know for sure it had anything to do with the boy. She was driving a patrol car. Someone could have been targeting our department in general or the sheriff in particular. Not everyone is in our corner when we arrest people."

"Tom's right." Liz grabbed hold of the lifeline Tom had just tossed. "It might not have anything to do with Jeremy."

Liz placed her hand gently on Sal's arm. "I know you're upset. But you saved me." She smiled into his eyes. "Thank you. You are a dear friend."

Their eyes locked and silent messages flashed between them.

An embarrassed flush, probably caused by his emotional overreaction, covered Sal's neck. She knew he was trying to save face when he nodded and started to turn away.

Suddenly, a deafening roar filled the air. The ground shook from the force of the explosion and a fireball shot at least fifty feet into the air.

Even though Liz stood on the ridge, she could still feel the heat from the bright orange-yellow flames that were turning her patrol car into liquid metal and ash. Thick, black, acrid smoke billowed through the air, filling her lungs, burning her eyes and causing her throat to spasm with violent coughs.

Grateful that she had been pulled from the vehicle in time, she couldn't help but wonder if her luck would hold next time. That uneasy sixth sense she'd come to rely on over the years sped along her nerve endings and twisted her gut into painful knots. Liz was certain that it wasn't *if* there'd be a next time—but *when*.

FIVE

"Lizzie."

Strong hands spun her around and she found herself cradled against a broad, rock-solid chest. She breathed in the tantalizing mix of spicy aftershave and maleness.

"It's going to be all right." Adam's voice rumbled against the top of her head and when he spoke his breath fanned through her hair like a welcome summer breeze.

For an instant, Liz allowed herself the luxury of accepting his comfort. She burrowed deeply into the warmth of his arms as if it were a restful cocoon from all harm. For just this one precious moment, she wasn't Sheriff Bradford needing to organize a crime scene. She wasn't a woman living with past hurts and unanswered questions. She was simply Lizzie—a woman cradled in the arms of a man who had once laughed with her, protected her and loved her.

His arms felt so good. Her cheek pressed against his chest reminded her of teenage years where a hug could last for hours and a kiss... She didn't think she would ever be able to forget the tenderness or feel of his kiss.

Then the moment passed. Time to come back to real life.

Gently, but with determination, she pushed against

his chest and stepped back. "Adam, I'd appreciate it if you'd check on Jeremy. He needs you right now."

She didn't wait for an answer or dare to look into his golden-brown eyes for fear she might not have the strength to turn away. She had loved this man with her whole heart—and he'd shattered it into a thousand pieces. She had no intention of giving him the chance to do it again.

She took a second to size up the situation, noting the fire trucks and additional state troopers who had arrived on the scene, the gridlock of parked cars as their occupants stood on the edge of the chaos, watching. She took control and stepped back into sheriff mode as if she hadn't missed a beat.

"Tom, I just saw Davenport pull up. I'll brief him on the current situation. I'd like you to start making your way through the crowd and see what you can find out. Maybe someone noticed someone running away from the scene."

"Yeah, let's hope they were carrying a high-powered rifle when it ain't hunting season. That would sew it up for us nice and neat."

"You never know who saw what until you ask, right? Go work your magic and I'll meet up with you later.

"Darlene, leave me your car. You can grab a ride back to the office with Sal. I want you to start going through the files and make a list of all our unhappy customers."

"That's going to be an awfully long list, Sheriff. I don't think any of our customers are too happy when we arrest them."

Liz smiled. "Granted. But I want you to pay attention to anyone we arrested that was particularly belligerent. Someone who reacted out of the norm. Don't overlook any family member that may have been particularly threatening, either. Remember, this doesn't have to be about Jeremy. The perp targeted a patrol car. This can be a nutcase bent on revenge against any one of us."

Liz turned toward Sal. Her eyes searched his, hoping that whatever feelings she thought she might have glimpsed earlier were now gone.

"Sal, I want you to take another long, hard look at the murder case you're working. Maybe the drug dealer had friends who don't like us stirring up a hornet's nest in their territory."

"Will do, boss." Sal offered a weak smile—saving face for a macho cop was difficult, for an Italian Romeo even harder. "Just as soon as you let the paramedics take a look at that leg."

Sal sounded just as cocky and sure of himself as always. She was grateful the awkwardness between them had passed. She didn't want to lose Sal as a friend or as a colleague. He was too valuable in both categories. She raised her hands in a gesture of surrender.

"Okay. I hear you. Now, get back to the office and let's see if we can't nip this thing in the bud. Maybe we've overlooked something. Maybe somebody thinks we know more about this dealer's murder than we do."

As soon as her team dispersed, Liz headed toward Davenport. It took only a few minutes to bring him up to speed on the events of the afternoon. She even spared a second to stop and talk with the fire chief. She requested any pertinent information be sent to her via email or cell phone and took the time to give him her contact information.

Finally, the throbbing in her leg won out. The ache had become sharp, shooting pain that stole her breath and she knew she couldn't put it off any longer. Grimacing, she limped over to the ambulance and poked her head inside.

Jeremy sat on the far end of the stretcher, his teddy bear clutched tightly against his chest. Adam, sporting a thick white bandage across the right side of his forehead, sat beside him.

When Jeremy spotted her, he became excited. He dropped his bear on his lap and flailed his hands. "Go home. Jeremy wants to go home."

One of the paramedics assisted Liz into the cramped quarters. She scooted toward the cab and sat on a small portable seat opposite the top of the gurney. Unable to resist, she reached out and gently brushed the child's sweaty, wet locks off his forehead. "I know, sweetheart. I want to go home, too."

"Jeremy go home." He pulled his bear to his chest and rocked in an unceasing rhythm.

"How is he?" Liz asked the paramedic crouched beside her.

"Better than you. That wound needs stitches. I need to get you to the hospital."

Liz never liked the sight of blood, let alone the sight of her own, and the wound made her feel suddenly lightheaded.

"No hospital. I'm fine." Black specks appeared in her line of vision and her stomach somersaulted at the lie. "Just bandage it up."

"You're not fine." Adam spoke for the first time. "You're stubborn, independent, hardheaded, but you're not fine. Let the man do his job and take care of that wound."

Liz bristled beneath the stern tone of his voice. "I certainly don't need you to tell me what to do, Adam Morgan." She glared at the paramedic as though his bringing up the subject of her wound was the cause of all their problems. "Now, answer my question. How is Jeremy?"

The two men glanced at each other. The paramedic shrugged as if to say, *I'm doing what she says. You deal with her.*

Before the paramedic could report his findings, Adam said, "Surprisingly, Jeremy's doing fine. He has a couple of bumps and bruises. He's confused—but so much has happened to him this week that I'm afraid that is becoming his new normal. He's exhausted from emotional stress. Otherwise, I think he told you exactly how he feels. Jeremy wants to go home."

Liz nodded. "Okay. That's what I needed to know." She started to stand and the interior of the ambulance swirled as if she were seeing it from the inside of a tornado funnel. She sat back down, closed her eyes and held her head in her hands.

Darlene stuck her head inside the ambulance. "Why don't I take Jeremy outside while you get that leg taken care of?" She had slipped a baseball jacket on over her uniform. Liz was grateful for her sensitivity to Jeremy's needs.

Adam looked Jeremy in the eyes and told him that Darlene was a friend and would be putting him in the car so they could go home. Surprisingly, the mention of going home this time seemed more important to Jeremy than anything else and he went willingly.

Darlene lifted the boy out of the ambulance. "I'll leave you my car and go back to the office with Sal as soon as you're finished in here."

"The paramedic can't stitch your leg," Adam said after the boy was gone. "You have to go to the hospital. You need a doctor."

Liz heard the self-satisfied tone in his voice and wanted to pitch something at him.

"I have a doctor—you."

"I'm a psychiatrist."

"Aren't psychiatrists medical doctors who special-ize in psychiatry?"

"I don't have what I need on board. Lizzie, go to the hospital."

"Ever hear of butterfly stitches?"

His sigh exposed his exasperation with her. "Let me take a look. If it's too deep, you'll need regular stitches."

"Just do the best you can, Adam. I am going to make sure Jeremy gets home safely and this investigation is organized before I waste valuable time sitting in an E.R. getting stitches. Pack it. Bandage it. Whatever. But I don't have time to waste right now."

Adam saw the determination in her eyes. He pulled his identification out of his wallet and showed it to the paramedic. "I'd appreciate it if you'd slide down and let me take a look at this wound."

The paramedic looked at the grim expression on the sheriff's face, grinned and jumped out the back of the wagon. He seemed quite happy not having to deal with the situation, but he didn't wander far in case he was needed.

Adam cut off the lower half of Liz's pant leg and rolled up the top, revealing her thigh. He cleaned the wound with peroxide and sprayed it with an antiseptic.

"You're lucky. It's nastier looking than it really is."

His touch was light and gentle, but as his fingers moved across her skin, a rush of sensation pulsed through her body. A flush of heat colored her neck and cheeks. It felt as though someone had suddenly cut off her oxygen supply.

He looked into her eyes and a ghost of a smile crossed his lips. She could tell that he knew what his touch was doing to her. Many things had changed over the years but their reaction to each other wasn't one of them. She was grateful when he broke eye contact and finished bandaging the wound.

His hand still cradled her thigh and Liz could barely stand the sensations racing through her body at his touch. The second he was finished, she pushed down the top of her pant leg, threw him a quick thank-you, and jumped out of the back of the vehicle.

Stubborn. Hardheaded. Beautiful. Vulnerable. Strong. A paradox if he'd ever run into one.

Liz was even more intriguing as a grown, independent woman than she'd been as the teenage girl he'd once loved. Adam knew that when he saw her again it would bring back past feelings, questions—and, yes, even pain—to the surface, but he'd thought he'd prepared for their encounter.

Fifteen years was a long time. He wasn't a boy anymore. He was an adult with all the physical and emotional needs of a man. He had devoted his adult professional years to helping other people understand and cope with their feelings, past hurts and pain so they could move on with their lives.

Seeing her again should have been a piece of cake. He'd expected an awkward moment or two and then a mutual acknowledgment of years past and a healthy acceptance of the present situation.

But he was wrong.

What he hadn't counted on was Lizzie.

Her love of life and outgoing personality filled whatever room she entered with an energy that couldn't be ignored. Everything he had loved about her then—her compassion for others, her sense of humor, her integrity, her sense of responsibility—had only grown and matured over the years.

Lizzie, draped protectively over a sleeping child. Lizzie, standing toe to toe with him, not afraid, not compromising her beliefs and forcing him to defend his therapy plan. Lizzie, in pain and trapped inside a vehicle, still in control and issuing orders to save others. Lizzie, bleeding, limping, frail.

Adam's throat closed and he swallowed a lump of unshed tears.

She was still his Lizzie—if only he could chip through that cold, hard, protective shell she'd built around her heart and show her how he felt.

Dear Lord, help me. How am I going to win back a woman who doesn't want to be won? I'll give it my all, Lord, but I'm afraid this time my all won't be enough. She's built her armor too strong, her protective wall too tall. Only You can soften her heart. Please, Lord, show me the way to gain her forgiveness. I can't bear losing her all over again.

"Adam?"

He heard a female voice call his name just seconds before eighty pounds of bounding yellow Lab jumped up on him.

"Down, Rerun." He hugged the dog and gently pushed his forepaws off his body and to the ground. Tousling the dog's fur, he raised his eyes in search of its owner. "Hi, Charlie."

"'Hi, Charlie'? That's all you have to say?"

He arched an eyebrow.

"The good Lord in Heaven must have been riding shotgun with you on this one." The petite redheaded woman reached out and touched the white gauze bandage on his forehead. "You're hurt."

Before Adam could utter a word, she threw herself at him and wrapped her arms tightly around his neck. "You big, dumb lummox. You could have gotten yourself killed."

Liz loudly cleared her throat and drew their attention.

Adam looked into Liz's eyes. He wasn't surprised to see the unspoken accusation lurking there. She'd made it painfully obvious from the moment he'd arrived back in town that nothing he said or did would be right with her.... But he wasn't prepared for the pain he saw in those pale blue eyes, as well. Was she jealous? Was it too much to hope that she could possibly still harbor feelings for him? Yes, it probably was. Not after all these years. Not after everything he'd done. All he'd seen so far was indifference and a chill that made him want to wear thermal underwear in August.

Adam reached up and unhooked the woman's arms from around his neck. He felt as guilty as a boy who had been caught with his hand in the cookie jar, even though he knew he didn't have a doggone thing to feel guilty about.

"Lizzie…"

Liz stepped forward and extended her hand to the woman. "I'm Sheriff Bradford."

They shook hands but not before Charlie sent a questioning glance his way. She'd picked up on the emotional undercurrents racing between him and the sheriff. She just hadn't figured out yet what they were.

"Hello, Sheriff. I'm Charlene Haddonfield. My friends call me Charlie." She reached down and patted the golden Lab lying patiently at her feet. "This is Rerun."

Liz's emotions slipped behind an unreadable mask. She locked her gaze with Adam's. "This is Charlie? This is the person who is moving into the house with you and Jeremy?"

Adam hurried to explain before she added one more transgression against him. "Charlie is moving into the house with *all* of us. She's been working with me off and on for years. She trains dogs and is working on a pilot program to provide support dogs for autistic children."

Liz smiled first at Charlie and then at Rerun. "May I pet him?"

"Yes. Thanks for asking. So many people approach guide dogs as though they were pets, not workers, and sometimes it gets confusing for the animal."

Liz crouched down toward the dog and grimaced as pain shot through her leg. The bleeding had stopped but the movement still hurt.

"Hello, boy. You're a handsome fellow. Yes, you are." Rerun wagged his tail enthusiastically but never moved from his position at Charlie's feet. Liz looked up at both of them. "Where's Jeremy? Has he seen him yet?"

Adam gestured to the open rear door of Darlene's patrol car. Jeremy was belted inside.

"He's seen him but doesn't want anything to do with the dog at the moment," Charlie said.

Liz shot her a questioning glance.

"Don't worry," Charlie said. "That's not unusual. The boy's been through enough today. We'll introduce them little by little after we get home."

Jeremy, who had looked like he hadn't been paying any attention to the adults, was listening to every word. "Home. Jeremy wants to go home."

The three adults chuckled.

Liz stood and opened the driver's door and slid behind the wheel. "Sounds good to me, Jeremy. Let's go home."

He crouched in the heavy brush and watched the scene unfold with interest. His hands trembled slightly when he raised the binoculars to his face. He wasn't sure whether the shaking was due to needing a fix or whether it was caused by the nonstop nagging voice of his conscience. Sure, things weren't happening the way he'd planned. He'd never intended to kill that kid's parents. He'd just wanted to square things with the dad.

One thing led to another and the whole mess blew up in his face.

He glanced over at what was left of the wreckage. The fire was out. The road had been reopened and the crowd had dispersed. The last of the fire trucks were rolling up their hoses and preparing to leave.

He hadn't wanted to shoot the tires out from under the sheriff's car, either. His conscience yelled long and loud about that one. But what choice did he have? He had to make sure that kid couldn't tell anyone what happened that night—not ever—even if it meant that others would become collateral damage.

He couldn't believe that all three of them made it out without more than some cuts and bruises. What kind of luck was that? Anyone else would have been killed in the wreckage either from the high speed of the crash or from the explosion.

He adjusted the zoom lens and brought the adults into focus.

Great! Now a woman and a dog had joined the party. This hole he'd dug for himself just kept getting deeper and deeper. What was he going to do now?

He slipped the binoculars into their case, backed up through the brush and made his way to his car. He had to gain control of the situation fast, before things got worse. He had to stop worrying about killing innocent people and just get the job done.

He wasn't a bad guy. It was just rotten circumstances—survival of the fittest—them or him. And when it came to survival, he knew one thing for certain. When all of this was said and done, he had every intention of being the last one standing. All he needed was to come up with a foolproof plan.

But first he needed a fix.

SIX

Liz turned up the graveled driveway and the breath caught in her throat when the white-pillared house appeared.

Please, Lord, don't let this be a bad idea. Please don't let our human errors hurt this child any more.

"Home. Home. Home." Jeremy's voice rose with excitement. He rocked forcefully back and forth in his car seat.

Liz eased to a stop right in front of the burgundy door. She turned off the ignition and just sat there, her heart hammering in her chest, her hands trembling.

Charlie pulled up behind them with Rerun crated in the back of her SUV but she, too, turned off the engine and waited.

Adam circled the vehicle and helped Jeremy out of his car seat. The boy ran, opened the door and raced inside.

Liz could hear Jeremy's voice drifting back through the open doorway.

"Mommy. Jeremy wants Mommy."

Her feet felt as if they were encased in cement but she forced herself to follow the child into the house. She stood in the foyer, unable to take another step.

Jeremy raced through the living room, dining room, study, kitchen, foyer and back again in a never-ending circle. Adam followed close behind. In each room, when he found it empty, Adam would get down on one knee, turn the boy's face so he could look the child in the eyes, and say, "Mommy and Daddy are together in Heaven. They are not coming back. But Jeremy is safe. Jeremy is going to be okay."

Jeremy would pull out of Adam's hold and race to the next room. "Mommy. Jeremy needs Mommy."

Adam followed close behind. In each room, he gave Jeremy a chance to search it. Then he'd kneel eye level with the child and repeat the same four sentences, always assuring Jeremy that he was safe and that he would be okay.

The child cried and ran from room to room, calling for a mother that couldn't answer, and Liz thought she was going to be sick to her stomach. Tears burned behind her eyes, and her throat constricted so tightly she was barely able to breathe. She almost hated Adam for the pain he was causing the child by bringing him here.

The ritual went on for hours. The child would calm down, be distracted by other things, like his exercise room or his computer, and then he'd stand up and start calling and looking again.

Adam never left the child's side. He kept his voice low and comforting. He kept his sentences short. He repeated the same sentences over and over again.

Finally, out of sheer exhaustion, Jeremy seemed to settle down. He'd stay for longer periods of time at his computer. He'd sit in his little rocker in the exercise room and hug his bear. He even ate a sandwich and piece of fruit that Charlie had prepared and brought upstairs.

Liz felt like a fish out of water and of no help. She

simply stood by and watched. She'd been right. They never should have brought the boy back to this house. Why hadn't she listened to her own instincts instead of trusting a man who had proved himself untrustworthy? Unable to watch the scene any longer, she went downstairs and sat in a chair on the front porch.

She'd called Sal and made sure the investigation was proceeding as requested. When he heard the break in her voice, he reminded her that she didn't have to go through with this. They could—and should—put the child in protective custody far, far away. A small part inside her wanted to do just that.

But another voice, a louder voice, wanted to believe that Adam could help Jeremy with both the loss of his parents and his memories of the trauma. She wanted to believe that more than anything else because this child was special. He made her feel things she didn't understand. Feelings she'd never had before—and didn't want to have. She was a career woman and had no room in her life or her heart for a child. Her brain knew it. Why didn't her heart?

Liz stared out into the darkness. The gentle summer night's breeze ruffled her hair and kissed her cheeks. It was a welcome relief after the stifling heat and humidity. Ordinarily, sitting here would be peaceful, enjoyable.

But not tonight.

Change was in the air and it wasn't just the weather.

A heaviness weighed on her shoulders. A deep, unsettling feeling crept up her spine and twisted her stomach into knots. These weren't rational feelings easily backed up with physical evidence. No one had warned her about a future problem. But something bad was coming. She felt it all the way down to her soul.

It wasn't what she saw or heard that caused the hair on the back of her neck to stand up and her spine to stiffen. It was what she didn't.

It was the stillness.

The absolute silence.

The presence of evil.

She wrapped her arms around herself as a chill skittered through her body. She didn't know who…or when…or how…but she'd be ready. She refused to let this innocent boy fall victim to any more pain.

Charlie told him that Liz had been outside for hours. Once he was certain that Jeremy was asleep for the night, he asked her to keep an ear out if Jeremy woke up, and he went downstairs.

Knowing only Charlie and Jeremy had eaten, he fixed a couple of sandwiches, some chips and sliced apples and carried them to the porch.

Liz had lit a half-dozen candles, which illuminated the area enough to see but wasn't as glaring a light as the porch lamp. It was still enough light to catch the angry expression on her face. He'd barely set a plate beside her and sat down before she attacked.

"I told you not to bring him here. I can't believe what you put that child through. That was torture!" Her voice rose and her eyes shimmered with unshed tears. "I don't know what ever made me think I could trust you."

He winced at her barb but understood her reason for it.

"Liz, Jeremy's going to be okay."

"What? You think if you follow me from room to room saying Jeremy's going to be okay that suddenly I will just believe it?"

He took a deep breath. How was he going to make

her understand? Ease her pain? Start to listen to the things he needed to say to her? Right now it was brick wall after brick wall.

"Jeremy's asleep in his own bed in his own room. Jeremy is okay."

She shot him a look of disbelief and disgust. "If Jeremy is asleep, it is because the child collapsed out of sheer exhaustion after everything that happened to him today."

He tried another tactic. "Try to eat. I made a sandwich for you. You haven't eaten all day." He nudged the plate to the edge of the table.

She stood up and shot another glare his way. "My relief gets here at eleven. Meanwhile, for your own safety, I suggest you go inside."

He looked deep into her eyes and wondered for a split second if he was in more danger from the bad guy or from her.

"I'm going to walk the perimeter. Don't be here when I get back."

He stared at her retreating back and prayed things would be easier in the morning.

Liz couldn't believe what a difference a couple of days made. She watched Jeremy and Rerun romp together in the backyard. It was hard to believe that this was the same child who had sobbed and run from room to room searching for his mother only three days ago.

Jeremy, who was rolling on the ground, poked and prodded Rerun in a lame attempt to keep the dog away. Rerun didn't seem to mind Jeremy's pushes and shoves. Instead, the dog used his head and snout to rock the boy back and forth on the lawn.

Jeremy seemed to be enjoying this game with his new

furry friend. The child's high-pitched giggles filled the air and brought a smile to Liz's face. She hadn't heard the boy laugh before and the sound played like a favorite song she wished would never end.

"I told you that you could trust Rerun. He knows what he's doing."

Liz turned and smiled at Charlie who leaned against the opposite door frame. "Good morning, Charlie." Liz reached out and accepted the mug of coffee Charlie offered. "Thanks." She took a sip of the hot liquid and hoped the caffeine would kick her energy level to high gear since right now it felt like she was operating on fumes.

"Figured you needed it. Sleep-deprived human beings usually do." Charlie shrugged and grinned. "But maybe you're not human at all. Three days ago, I pegged you for superwoman status. Setting up an office in the house. Running a police station remotely yet still staying on top of investigations and officers and yet never taking your eyes off of Jeremy…or Adam and I."

Heat flooded Liz's cheeks at the inference, but she just sipped her coffee and remained silent.

"But maybe instead of superwoman you are really superhuman. You might be an alien hiding out in human skin. What do you say?" Charlie grinned wider, as though pleased with herself, and took a sip from her own cup.

Liz chuckled. "You never can tell. I don't feel very human this morning, that's for sure."

"Jeremy, don't hit," Charlie yelled out to Jeremy. "No hitting."

Jeremy pretended he didn't hear but both women noticed his pushes and shoves subtly turned into pats and hugs. When it was evident the dog was in no danger of being hurt, she relaxed back against the door frame.

"It's good to hear him laugh, isn't it?" Charlie nodded in Jeremy's direction. "No sweeter sound for sure."

Liz's heart clenched. Almost from the moment she'd found the child huddled beneath the pile of blankets in his mother's closet, all she had wanted to do was hold the boy in her arms, rock him, kiss him and not let anyone or anything ever hurt him again. She didn't understand why these maternal feelings had rushed to the surface. She'd been with sick children, injured children and abused children before. She'd felt empathy for their situation but she'd never felt such deep personal emotion. She wasn't sure why and she definitely didn't know what to do about it.

"The poor kid hasn't had much to laugh about lately, has he?" Charlie smiled at her over the rim of her coffee. "But that seems to be changing. Adam is doing a wonderful job with him. Don't you think?" Before Liz could answer, she said, "Jeremy is taking to Rerun quicker than I expected, too. I think the two of them are a good match."

"Thanks, Charlie. I appreciate all you've done for Jeremy the past couple of days."

"Don't thank me. I'm only doing what Adam hired me to do. Maybe you should thank him." She gestured inside with her mug and then stepped off the porch to join the dog and the boy on the lawn.

Liz remained in the doorway and watched the scene in front of her a little longer. She watched as Charlie sat cross-legged beside Jeremy. She petted Rerun and encouraged the boy to pet not push. She had infinite patience and always wore a smile on her face. Jeremy liked Charlie, Liz could tell. He quieted down in her presence. He echoed her sentences and followed most of her requests.

Liz liked Charlie, too.

She had to admit she hadn't when they first met. The petite redheaded beauty represented all the gals in high school that Liz had always wished she could be and never was. The cheerleaders. The prom queens. The tiny, doll-like, curvy females that Liz towered over. She remembered tons of times she'd tried to bargain with God. She begged him to please let her stop growing taller than many men, to please let her have wider hips and a smaller waist.

But God had other plans.

Liz grew to five-eleven and had a thick waist and narrow hips. Her mother had told her a hundred times that she was lucky she was slender, lithe, athletic. But she hadn't ever felt lucky. All she'd wanted was to be one of the pretty little Barbie gals. She was angry and sorely disappointed when God's answer was no.

Thinking those painful adolescent years were way behind her, Liz was caught off guard when they surfaced again the first time she set eyes on Charlie. It was all she could do to stifle the unexpected tsunami of jealousy that swept over her when she saw Charlie's arms wrapped around Adam's neck. Fifteen years ago or not, she still wasn't pleased to see another woman in Adam's arms. She was fully prepared to dislike her with a passion.

But no one could dislike Charlie—not even her.

"Penny for your thoughts."

A warm shiver raced up and down her spine at the sound of Adam's voice. She could almost feel the touch of his breath on the back of her neck. She wanted to lean against the rock-hard wall of his chest and tuck his arms around her. But sanity prevailed. *Been there. Done that. Ain't doing it again. Hurts too much when it's over.*

"Morning, Adam. You're up early."

"Could say the same about you. That is, if you slept in the first place. I thought I heard you moving around until the wee small hours. Want to talk about what's troubling you?"

"Nothing's troubling me. I just have a lot on my mind. It hasn't been easy trying to run my office from here. You know I'm smack-dab in the middle of several murder investigations."

"Sure that's all it is?"

She laughed humorlessly. "Isn't that enough?" Adam smiled, took a sip of his coffee and waited for her to speak. How did he do that? He seemed to be able to see beyond the surface. Most people accepted what she said at face value. Adam peered deeper.

"I must admit that it's been difficult sleeping in the master bedroom," Liz said. "Surrounded by the remnants Kate and Dave's life. My mind fills with thoughts of the terror and fear of their last moments. From what I can ascertain from the evidence, they knew they were going to die—and their actions weren't ones of escape or survival. They both were focused on saving and protecting their son."

"That's what good parents do. They protect their children."

Liz's thoughts flashed to her dad, her childhood and Luke. She loved her father but he had been far from perfect. Protect them? Sure, he protected them from the world. But who protected them from him?

"Speaking of dads, how is your father these days?" Liz looked at him with genuine interest. She hadn't heard a word, not even a whisper, about the Morgans after they moved away.

"Mom and Dad are fine. They have a place overlooking Central Park in New York. They retired early and plan to enjoy their lives. Last I spoke to them, they're flying to Hawaii for a month."

Liz smiled. "Must be nice. Psychiatry can be a lucrative business, I suppose."

"It can be." Adam shrugged. "It's also given me an opportunity to pay it back, help people I wouldn't have been able to help otherwise."

She'd read about his mentoring programs and his generosity to various social agencies.

This was a mature side of Adam. Philanthropist. Stellar professional reputation. Impressive. But what surprised her the most was his way with children. His kindness. His patience. His innate ability to know when to be stern and when it was okay to be permissive. He'd make a wonderful father.

She couldn't believe she was even entertaining such thoughts. Where was all this coming from? Adam as a good father. Maternal feelings toward Jeremy. This case was rocking her carefully built world and she'd be happy when it was over.

But even if she was devoted to her career, she was still a woman, wasn't she?

Her eyes traveled across the darkened stubble of his unshaved face. Liz had to physically fight the urge to drag her fingers across the roughened surface of his cheek. The stubble lent an air of "bad boy" mystique to the man. Then again, that's what he was, wasn't he? A bad boy who broke her heart and disappeared without an explanation?

"Are you all right, Lizzie?" He tilted his head and

studied her face with an intensity that melted her feet to the concrete.

She smiled up at him, her voice teasing. "I told you not to call me Lizzie."

He grinned—a slow, easy, inviting grin.

"And just how do you intend to stop me, huh?" He put his hand on the door frame just inches from her face and leaned his body closer. His eyes traced a slow path down every crest and curve of her body and back up again. His lips came so close to hers she could barely control the need to lean forward and steal a taste.

"What are you gonna do, Lizzie?" He drawled her name out slow and easy, his hot breath fanning her face. Teasing her. Tempting her. He slid an index finger down her cheek and moved it ever so slowly along the curve of her neck.

"Gonna arrest me, ma'am? Gonna put those nice silver handcuffs on my wrists?"

She grabbed his wrist, spun him around and slammed him against the door frame as if he were a perp she was arresting. She pinned him with her body, her leg planted firmly between the backs of his legs.

"Is this what you want?" she asked, whispering the words tantalizingly slow and soft against his ear. "I'll be glad to oblige with those handcuffs, you know. Anytime."

A deep rumbling laugh sounded in his throat.

"Okay, okay. I give up. You've proved your point."

Blood pounded through her body in a heated flush and left the telltale signs of her reaction to him on her reddened neck and cheeks. This was a side of Adam she'd never seen before. He was a grown man now— a dark, dangerous, fantastically attractive man.

And she was flirting with him. Was she crazy?

She released him and took a step back.

"I'm too busy to play word games with you, Dr. Morgan. In the past three weeks, in case you hadn't noticed, Country Corners has exploded from a sleepy little Midwest town to the hub of three homicide investigations, a car explosion and a town with a growing drug problem. It doesn't allow a sheriff much time for...anything."

Adam didn't try to argue with her, but his eyes and body language let her know he wasn't buying her explanation.

"Speaking of work, I have to get back to it." Liz tried to slip past him but his arm shot out and blocked her path. He held her gaze.

"Still think I made a mistake bringing the boy here?"

They both knew the first day had been torture. Each time she had shot him a glaring look, his eyes told her he knew exactly how she felt but still disagreed with her position. They'd barely said two words to each other in the past seventy-two hours.

But he was asking now. Her opinion seemed to really matter to him.

"I'm withholding judgment for now." She tried to move past him again but his arm still blocked the way.

"The boy's doing better. He's starting to adjust to his new normal, don't you think?"

She knew what he was asking. Would she be able to admit that maybe he'd been right? Or would her pride get in the way? Would she be able to accept Adam's professional decisions or would she continue to compare him to his father? Would she be able to stop dwelling on the tragic circumstances of her brother's death and see Jeremy's circumstances for what they were?

Adam never voiced those questions but they were

there—hidden in the depths of those beautiful, golden-brown, penetrating eyes.

Before she could answer, the phone rang.

"Excuse me." Liz pushed his arm aside and hurried into the house. She answered on the third ring.

"Sheriff Bradford."

"I think we found someone you might like to chat with, Sheriff. Do you remember Danny Trent?" Sal's voice sounded like the cat that swallowed the canary.

"Danny Trent? How could I forget wife-beating drunk Danny Trent?

"If I remember correctly, you picked him up but didn't arrest him," Liz replied.

"Not for lack of trying. When the wife realized we were going to lock up her boxing buddy and throw away the key, she jumped on my back and pummeled the life out of me."

Liz laughed. "I remember. She rode your back like you were a bucking bronco. I ended up arresting her for assaulting an officer."

"Don't I know it. She spent the night in a jail cell. He spent the night bending an elbow at Smitty's telling all his cronies about it. I hate domestic calls."

Liz laughed again. "Poor Sal. It's going to take you a while to live that one down. But I was proud of you. You never once raised your hand to her even though she did rip out a chunk of that beautiful, thick black hair of yours."

"Humph."

"And you think I'd want to talk to him why…?"

"Because he threatened to kill you…all of us really… if we didn't let his wife loose."

"So? He was drunk and the incident was almost a

week ago. You don't need me. You can do the interrogation."

"Trust me, boss. I really think you'll want to do this one."

She paused and considered her options. She trusted Sal implicitly. If he wanted her to drive into town, there had to be a good reason behind it.

"Okay, send Paul out here to relieve me. I'll come in as soon as he arrives."

"He's already on the way."

"Think you're calling the shots, do you? Smart aleck. Okay, I'll give you this round. I'll be in shortly but I still don't understand why. It's been my experience that wife beaters are nothing but cowards, anyway. He probably doesn't even remember what he said that night."

"You're right about men who beat women being cowards. But I asked around at a couple of the local bars. The guy hasn't let it rest. He's still running his mouth about how he's going to make you pay. Teach you what it would be like for you to go up against a real man."

"Yeah, right. Real man, huh?" She sighed. Sometimes human nature didn't seem worth the trouble and she wondered why God just didn't turn His back on the whole mess. How could He still love and forgive people who made such bad choices over and over again? But He did. She wondered if she'd ever be able to comprehend the depths of God's love.

"I know you, Sal. There's got to be more to this or you wouldn't be wasting my time. What aren't you telling me?"

Liz heard a self-satisfied chuckle on the other end of the line.

"Darlene ran a complete background check on him. He's ex-military. Before he was dishonorably discharged, he was a sniper."

SEVEN

Liz entered the interrogation room. "As I live and breathe, it's Mr. Trent. Didn't think I'd be seeing you again so soon."

Danny's hands were folded together on top of the table. He looked up and glared at her. "I shouldn't be here. I didn't do anything. You have no right to haul me in here and treat me like this."

"That so?" Liz sat down opposite him. "Seems to me, you've been a very busy boy this past month. Two drunk and disorderly calls at Smitty's, one pending DUI charge and, oh yes, another 911 call for domestic abuse. But no charges on that one, right?"

Danny Trent filled the room with expletives.

Liz laughed. "That's all you got? Schoolboy foul language and blustering?"

He started to rise and Sal pushed him back down in his chair. "Don't move." Sal leaned over and got in his face. "I'm itching for a chance to show you what the right hook you gave your wife feels like. Just give me a reason."

Sal moved back but stayed close.

"What do you want?" Danny's sneer revealed yellowed teeth and poor dental hygiene.

Liz positioned herself out of the range of his breath. She shuffled some of the papers in the file in front of her. "We ran a little background check on you. Guess what we found?"

Danny leaned back in his chair and folded his arms across his chest.

"It's your party. I don't know and frankly I don't care."

Liz smiled and tapped her fingers on the manila folder. "It says you served five years in the army."

"Tell me something I don't know."

"You were a trained sniper. Pretty good at your job, too. Got yourself a couple of commendations."

"Yeah, so what? That was a long time ago."

"So, what I'd like to know is how does a decorated soldier get himself dishonorably discharged?"

Liz watched the man's ruddy complexion redden more. His body tensed.

"That's none of your dog-tailed business. What are you fishing around in my past for, anyway?"

"Answer her question." Sal glared at the suspect.

Liz picked up a sheet of paper, pretended to read and then smiled sweetly. "Mr. Trent, where were you three days ago at four-thirty in the afternoon?"

"Again, lady, none of your business."

Sal slapped the table. "Answer her question or I'm going to make it my business."

Danny slid a glance at Sal, seemed to realize the truth behind Sal's words and then turned his attention back to Liz.

"I was at work."

"Not true, Mr. Trent. We checked with your boss. Your time card shows you clocked out before lunch on Monday. So, where'd you go?"

He looked puzzled for a minute. "Oh yeah, I forgot. I ate something that didn't agree with me. I felt sick so I left."

"You were hungover, you mean."

Danny glared at her but remained silent.

"Okay, so you felt sick, couldn't work and clocked out. Where'd you go?"

"Home. Where you think? Ask my wife, she'll tell you."

"You see, that's a funny thing. We did just that and you know what? She said you were at work all day on Monday. Didn't come home until dinnertime." Liz folded her forearms on the table and leaned in a little closer. "So, where were you? This time try telling me the truth."

He eyes darted around the room as though searching for a hasty exit and he squirmed in his seat.

"I want a lawyer."

"Do you need a lawyer?"

"I didn't do anything. Why did you haul me in here? Charge me with something or let me get out of here."

Danny seemed to think if he shouted really, really loud that she'd cower and back down. It probably was how his wife reacted to his outbursts. Instead, Liz leaned in closer and smiled as sweetly and femininely as possible.

"What's the matter, Mr. Trent? I'm just a simple female asking you a simple question. Now you can handle that, can't you? Or do we need to call in a lawyer to hold your hand because you're not man enough to talk to me."

His eyes widened and he slammed his fists on the table. "I'm not afraid of any woman and I sure am not afraid of you."

Liz went for the kill. "Good for you. Now prove it.

Tell me why a decorated soldier was drummed out of service. Tell me where you were and what you were doing Monday afternoon." Liz got in his face almost nose to nose and made her voice stern and harsh. "Tell me. Now."

Something was scaring Danny and she knew it wasn't her. He twitched and twisted in his seat so much Liz was certain he'd burn a patch off his jeans. What was he hiding? She decided to try another tactic.

"That's what I thought. The man talks big but that's all it is…a whole lot of hot air. He's not man enough to answer my questions. Get him out of here, Sal. And check that seat. He probably wet himself when I got too close."

Danny Trent let out a roar, called her a colorful dirty word and lunged across the table. He grabbed Liz around the throat and squeezed. Before Sal could clear the edge of the table, Liz had propelled herself backward, pulling with all her strength. She used both her hands to come up between his arms and force his hands off her throat. He slid to the floor and in one fast, fluid motion, she had him rolled onto his stomach, his hands pinned behind his back and her knee slammed into the small of his back.

She yanked harder on his wrists. "Are you ready to play nice or am I going to have to cuff your cowardly butt and throw you in jail?"

Not waiting for an answer, she and Sal hauled him to his feet and returned him to his side of the table. She stood an inch taller than Danny and, for once, was grateful that she could use her height to intimidate a man. "Look, you little weasel, you have one minute to make a choice. You can sit your butt back down in that chair and answer my questions or Sal will lock you up for assaulting an officer so fast you won't have time to utter the word 'lawyer.' Your choice, buddy. What's it going to be?"

Danny Trent sat down. He threw a defeated look their way. "If I answer your questions, can I get out of here?"

"Maybe." She walked around the table and sat back down facing him. "But I guarantee that the only place you are going is to a jail cell if you don't."

She saw the bravado seep out of him like a balloon with a leak. His shoulders slouched and his eyes registered defeat.

"They threw me out of the army because I got hooked on drugs." He hung his head and, for the first time, he looked as if he was truly feeling remorse. "I've got a bad habit. I've tried to kick it but I can't. Sometimes when I'm high I hate myself. I get angry. Lose control." His voice dropped. "Hit my wife." He looked back and forth between them. "You think I want to hit her? I love Cathleen."

"Love, huh? Funny way of showing it, with your fists." Sal shook his head and made a sound of disgust.

"Where were you Monday, Mr. Trent?" Liz saw telltale glistening in his eyes and, for a moment, truly felt empathy for the man who had once been an exemplary soldier and was now a hard-core addict.

"I left work because I needed a fix." He looked up and self-loathing registered in his eyes. "I got what I needed."

Liz threw a hard stare his way. She didn't know yet what she was going to do with Danny Trent—or if she was looking at the sniper who had tried to kill her.

Liz glanced at her watch. Eight o'clock. Total darkness surrounded her, the headlights of her car the only illumination on the dirt road. The trees on either side stood like shadowed sentinels and blocked her view of the starlit evening sky. That deep-rooted uneasiness raised its ugly head and skittered along her spine.

Why had Adam insisted on bringing the boy back here? She understood that it was part of therapy, part of familiarity, structure and routine for Jeremy. But at what cost? The house sat smack-dab in the middle of the woods. Neighbors few and far between. A security nightmare. This was crazy. Why on earth had she gone against her own instincts and allowed it?

A wave of relief washed over her when she spotted the lights of the house through the trees. For a split second, she felt she was coming home, not to the house, but to the people inside—to Adam and Jeremy and even Charlie and Rerun—and it caused a deeper uneasiness than even the darkened woods.

She parked at the side of the house.

Paul must have heard her car. He was standing on the porch as she got out of her car and approached the house.

"Quiet on the home front, Paul?"

"Yes, ma'am."

"Thanks, Paul. I'm sorry I'm so late. You must be hungry. You can leave now. Grab yourself some dinner and have a good night."

"Oh, I'm not hungry, ma'am. Adam fixed us a big dinner."

"Adam cooked dinner?"

"Yep. Haven't had home cooking like that since I visited my mom in June. I'm stuffed." His face split into a wide grin and he patted his stomach.

"Really? Somehow I didn't picture Dr. Morgan as a great cook."

"Take my word for it, ma'am. He is. There was nothing but empty plates and full stomachs around that table."

Liz chuckled. "Good. I'm glad you didn't have to starve to death waiting for me to get back. You can leave now. Get a good night's rest. And thanks, Paul."

"No problem, Sheriff. Anytime you need someone to pull supper detail, you can call on me."

"That's good to know." She watched her deputy pull away and then let herself into the house. Immediately she punched in the security code on the pad inside the door so she wouldn't set off the alarm.

The house was quiet. The hall light upstairs was on and she saw another light coming from the downstairs study. When she reached the library door, she saw Adam sitting in one of the leather high-backed chairs beside an unlit fireplace.

Her eyes glanced over the floor-to-ceiling bookcases. She imagined that on a cold winter night it would seem like a slice of heaven to curl up here and read a book by a roaring fire. But tomorrow was Labor Day, the hot, humid days of August barely passed, and she was surprised to find him here. But then again, Adam was filled with surprises.

"Hi. How'd it go?" Adam closed the book he'd been reading and gave her his full attention. "Did you catch the bad guy?"

She threw herself into the leather chair opposite him. "I caught *a* bad guy but I'm still not sure that it's our bad guy. Not enough evidence to hold him but we're keeping a close eye on him. He's high on our suspect list. I'm sorry I'm so late."

"No problem. Paul did a fine job keeping an eye on things. He even baked cupcakes with Jeremy for our picnic tomorrow."

"Picnic? What picnic?"

"It's Labor Day. I'm having a barbecue."

"No, you're not. That will be a security nightmare. Whatever made you think you could have a barbecue—particularly without asking me?"

"Oh, I don't know." He crossed the room and playfully tapped the end of her nose. "Maybe because the barbecue is for all the law enforcement officers who have been laboring to keep us safe. Some of Davenport's men have accepted the invitation. But, mostly, it will be your team and the four of us. And, yes, I told them big, bulky flowered shirts over uniforms are a must."

Liz smiled and nodded her approval. "So, where is everyone? The house is pretty quiet."

"I just put Jeremy to bed a few minutes ago. He should be asleep by now. The last time I looked, Rerun was sprawled out across him."

"Ouch. Isn't the dog a little heavy to be on top of a five-year-old?"

Adam laughed. "Not for Jeremy. Remember, he responds to deep pressure not light touch."

Liz smiled. "Yeah, I guess Rerun is acting like a living, breathing swaddling blanket. Good dog." Liz glanced over her shoulder. "Speaking of good dog, where's his trainer? I haven't seen Charlie anywhere."

"After you left, I gave her the afternoon off. She drove into St. Louis for some retail therapy and said something about trying to squeeze in dinner and a movie."

Liz's breath took a hiccup. They were alone in the house. For the first time in fifteen years, it would be just the two of them. She didn't know how she felt about this unexpected turn of events. She just knew that her pulse quickened and her heart definitely skipped every third beat.

"You look tired." The deep timbre of his voice slid over her nerve endings and made every one of them stand up and take notice.

"I am." She tried to remain calm and not let him see how the thought of a solitary evening together was affecting her.

"I bet you didn't take the time to grab yourself anything to eat, did you?"

"I'll be fine. Go back to your book. I'll slip into the kitchen and fix myself a sandwich and then I've got some reports to look over. Sergeant Davenport's man should be here at eleven to take over the night shift."

Liz made a hasty exit to the kitchen. She barely made it to the refrigerator before she heard Adam's voice behind her.

"There's a dish for you in the microwave. I'll fix you a salad to go with it."

They were alone in the house. He'd kept dinner for her. This was stuff she'd thrown around in her mind about a thousand times when she'd played her what-if games. What if Adam had never left? What if they'd gotten married like they used to talk about? What if they had a quiet little house in the woods with their own child asleep upstairs? What if memories weren't painful and dreams did come true?

Her eyes burned and her hand clasping the door handle trembled. She stared at the covered plate as if it were a snake poised to strike.

How could this be happening to her? She didn't want a relationship, didn't need a relationship. She liked her life just the way it was. Why didn't he just go away before he messed things up—again.

Adam's hands clasped her shoulders. "Here, let me get it for you. You've been burning a candle at both ends. It won't hurt to take a breather." He steered her toward the kitchen counter.

Liz perched on a stool and watched him go to work. Within minutes, he'd set a place mat and utensils in front of her, made a salad and poured her a tall glass of iced tea. At the ding from the microwave, he donned an oven mitt and with exaggerated flourish whisked the plate in front of her.

"Voilà. An Adam Morgan specialty. Enjoy." Adam lifted the lid and waved the aroma of hot, steamy beef and noodles her way.

Liz almost salivated like Pavlov's dog and her stomach growled on cue.

Adam sat on a stool opposite her. He propped his elbows on the counter, held his head in his hands and had the silliest grin on his face, obviously in anticipation of the glowing accolades he expected to come his way.

Liz nibbled a small bite. As much as she didn't want to pump up his ego with exclamations about his genius in the kitchen, the second bite did her in. This was absolutely delicious.

"This is good."

"'Good'?" He waggled his eyebrows and waited for her to lavish more praise.

Liz laughed. "Okay, this is delicious. This is the most tender, moist beef I have ever tasted. Happy now?"

"Absolutely." He poured himself a glass of iced tea. "Just wait until you taste my beef, shrimp and chicken kebabs on the grill tomorrow. My special marinating sauce is so good I should patent it. Now go ahead. Eat."

He sat across from her and grinned ear to ear.

"What? Are you going to sit there and stare at me eating?"

Adam chuckled. "No. I'm going to sit here and keep you company while you're eating. Maybe have some adult conversation since I've been cooped up in the house with a five-year-old all day."

Liz swallowed slowly, trying to savor every bite. "'Adult conversation'? What? Didn't Paul fit that bill?"

Adam lifted his glass and gave her a mock salute. "Touché. But Paul kept himself pretty busy walking the perimeter of the house until a moat started to form."

Liz almost spit out her mouthful of iced tea as she suppressed a laugh.

"It wasn't until I found out he loves baking that I was able to encourage him to come inside. Besides…" Adam's voice deepened and he caught her gaze with his. "He isn't as pretty to look at as you are."

The blood raced to her face and Liz felt the heated flush of her skin. Her stomach fluttered and her pulse thumped like a racehorse in the final stretch. It took her a moment to respond and when she did she tried to put things back on an even keel.

"I bet you say that to all the girls. You need to work on that, Adam. Your cooking is fabulous. Your pickup lines, not so good." She stood up. "Thanks so much for saving dinner for me. Now if you'll excuse me, I really do need to work on those reports."

She reached out for her empty plate.

His hand captured her wrist. He smiled up at her and her heart flip-flopped in her chest. His eyes were intense and endearing.

"You've been working all day. Don't you think you deserve a little downtime?" Ever so softly he rubbed the tender skin of her wrist with his thumb.

A comfortable tension, an undercurrent of awareness, filled the air between them. It would be so easy to relax and see where the evening led. But she couldn't afford to make the same mistakes again. She had to keep her guard up with Adam, even though it was getting harder and harder to do so.

"You can't run away forever, Lizzie. Sooner or later we are going to have to talk."

"We have nothing to talk about, Adam. What happened to us happened too many years ago to bother with. I've moved on and I'm sure you have to."

With his other hand, he reached up and gently stroked her cheek.

"I still have feelings for you, Lizzie. And I'm hoping you have feelings for me, too...just buried."

The breath caught in her throat. What? Were there no telephones in his world? No post offices? No homing pigeons? No skywriting? No way in existence to communicate with her at any time over the past fifteen years and apologize for shattering her world into a million pieces?

How many times had she wanted to hear him say that she mattered? How many months after he'd left had she lain awake at night and prayed it was all a bad dream?

Now he sat in this kitchen and told her that he had unresolved *feelings* for her?

Instead of angering her, it just made her feel sad.

"I hurt you," Adam said, his voice filled with regret. "I know that and I'm so, so sorry."

She eased her wrist from his grasp.

"Thank you for your apology, Adam. I appreciate it. I do. But an apology doesn't turn back the clock and make everything okay. You of all people should know that."

"You're still holding on to your anger? You can't

find it in yourself to forgive me and give me a second chance?"

"I forgave you long ago, Adam. I continue to forgive you, and anyone else who ever wronged me, every morning when I recite the Lord's Prayer."

Hope flashed in his eyes.

"But I'm not interested in exploring a relationship with you."

She saw his disappointment and it tugged at her heart.

"This has nothing to do with our past. This is all about the present. I like my life. I'm good at what I do and I'm happy doing it."

"What does that have to do with spending time together? Getting to know one another again and seeing if there's anything there worth rekindling?"

"Because I'm married, Adam—to my job. And I like it that way."

She smiled into his eyes and found herself wishing that things could be different. But they couldn't. Not now. Not ever.

"I'm not giving up." He grinned at her and waggled his eyebrows. "Just saying…"

"Good night, Adam. Thanks for the dinner." She felt his eyes on her back as she walked away.

EIGHT

Liz sat at the head of the dining room table. "Thank you, gentlemen, for meeting with me here. I realize this isn't easy for any of you."

"Where's the boy?" Tom Miller looked over his shoulder. "I don't want him to come in and see me dressed in my uniform and freak out. I'm not coming to your barbecue. I'm on duty today and didn't want to have to drive all the way home to change."

Liz smiled. "Don't worry about it. Dr. Morgan and Charlie are working with him in the backyard. You'll be gone long before he's scheduled to come back inside."

"He has a schedule for when he can come in and out of the house?" Sergeant Davenport shifted his weight in his chair. "Does it work? My wife and I could barely keep our kids out of juvenile hall let alone worry about how often they came in and out of the house."

"I still think the best thing for everyone, including the kid, would have been to put him in the witness protection program and ship him off somewhere." Sal folded his arms over his chest and waited for her to argue with him.

Liz smiled, chose to ignore his remark and answered Davenport. "Autistic children thrive best with behavior modification and a daily structured schedule. Jeremy responds well to structure. This is his exercise time. He won't be coming in for at least an hour. So, let's get started, shall we?"

Sergeant Davenport spoke first. "We've exhausted any leads we had regarding the Hendersons' life before they moved here. They lived a squeaky-clean middle-class existence. Worked hard. Seemed to have a solid family life. Didn't draw any unnecessary attention to themselves. Certainly not enough to have someone follow them here and execute them."

"How about you, Tom? Anything?"

"Which investigation you asking about, Sheriff? The drug dealer found behind Smitty's bar? The Henderson homicides? The car explosion?"

Liz shook her head and chuckled. "Okay, Tom, I hear you. Overworked and underpaid. I get it. If you have any information for the team on anything, we'd like to hear it."

"Yeah, well, I suffered through a couple of afternoon teas with the local gossips and it wasn't easy, I'm telling you."

Snickers were heard from the other men at the table, but no one interrupted.

"Heard that there was some bad blood between Henderson and the Third National Bank manager."

Liz twirled her pen in her fingers and chewed her bottom lip. This was definitely news to her. "What kind of bad blood?"

"Don't know for sure. That's the trouble with gossip. Gossip ain't accurate. But it seems that one of the tellers went around town telling tales of a loud argument Henderson had with the bank manager a few days before he was killed. The teller seems to think the bank manager and one of the other tellers was having an affair."

"Okay. Even if that were true, what would it have to do with Dave?"

Tom shrugged. "Everybody knows that the bank manager, Joe Grimes, is married. Rumor has it that the wife was a good friend of Henderson's wife. The word on the street is that Henderson told Grimes to end the affair or he'd spill the beans to Grimes's wife. According to the teller, Grimes was pretty burned up about it. Walked around the bank grumbling under his breath like a bear with a sore paw."

Sal spoke up. "Dirty thing, cheating on your spouse. Looks like Grimes is living up to his name." Chuckles and grimaces at the bad pun circled the table. "I get it. To a man of Henderson's religious beliefs, cheating on your wife is a no-no. But even if Henderson spilled the beans to the wife, in this day and age, I don't see that as a strong enough motive for Grimes to kill him."

"Maybe it isn't about the affair at all." Paul leaned forward, resting his forearms on the table. "Dave Henderson worked on computers, right? He worked on our computers the week before he died. Maybe he worked on the bank's computers, too. Maybe he saw somebody messing with the books or something."

"Wow, it's looking like this Joe Grimes might really be a suspect." Darlene made eye contact with Liz. "He was either cooking the books or cheating on his wife or maybe both, but either way he had big secrets he didn't want anyone to find out. But was it worth killing for?"

"Maybe. Maybe not." Tom shrugged. "Grimes married into money. Huge money. Anybody ever hear about something called a prenup? Mrs. Grimes set up an iron-clad one of those doohickeys. If Mr. Grimes was found fooling around, Mrs. Grimes wouldn't just kick him to the curb— She'd make sure he didn't have a penny in his pocket when she did."

Sal whistled. "That changes things. It gives Grimes at least twenty million reasons to want to keep Dave Henderson quiet, doesn't it?"

"Good work, Tom. Invite Mr. Grimes and his infamous teller to the station for a conversation. Sal, why don't you take a shot at both interviews?" Liz looked around the table. "Anyone have anything else?"

Sal spoke up. "I found out the names of two disgruntled employees that Henderson fired for one reason or another. That's worth looking into."

Liz nodded in agreement. "That it?" When no one commented, she stood.

"Okay, guys, that's it for today. Thanks again for driving out here. And thanks for not wearing uniforms. Unless something new develops, tomorrow we'll do a phone conference but for now I hear there's a pretty good barbecue starting in the backyard."

"I baked three dozen cupcakes. Be sure to try them." Paul beamed.

"Wuss."

Although it was an under-his-breath mutter, Liz still heard Tom. She stopped behind his chair and leaned down so only he could hear her speak. "I won't tolerate bullying in my department, Tom. Have I made myself clear?"

"I'm not bullying nobody. But a deputy baking cupcakes for a picnic? Your father would turn over in his grave."

"The majority of the great chefs and bakers in this world are men, Tom. How about if you get back to work and leave that lousy attitude at home."

Tom pushed away from the table and stormed out.

Liz followed the men to the back door but stopped Sal before he could go outside.

"Sal, something doesn't feel right to me. Those drugs we found under the mattress. Were they Dave's? Possible, yes. Probable, not really. I just don't buy it."

"Not all Christians are the good people they're supposed to be, boss."

"I realize that. People remain human even after they're saved and they can slip back into old ways and make mistakes."

Sal waited for her to make her point.

"But Sergeant Davenport didn't turn up even a sniff of illegal activity or drug use in the years before Henderson moved to Country Corners. Have you been able to tie Dave to any of the suspected drug dealers in town? Have you gone over his phone records with a fine-tooth comb? Any video surveillance outside the bars or anywhere else downtown that might have shown Dave meeting someone he shouldn't?"

"Darlene and Paul are going over the camera footage. But there's not much of it, boss. After all, this is Country Corners, not New York or even St. Louis. Not too many surveillance cameras to pull from."

"I understand." She continued to chew on her lower lip. "You know, Paul made a valid point. Dave had access to several high-profile computer systems in town— the bank, our office. I'm sure he's even done work at the church and for Trust Insurance. Maybe he did see something he shouldn't have. We need to check out that angle."

"Will do, boss."

"How about the first murder investigation? Any leads on that one?"

"Just a suspicion, boss, nothing concrete."

She arched an eyebrow.

"Don't worry. I'll tell you when I have something solid."

Liz smiled. "Okay, Sal. Go work your magic. I really need a miracle here."

"I didn't think miracles were in my job description, boss. But a little bird told me you have frequent conversations with the one that does handle those things. Maybe it's time for a little chat with that guy." Sal grinned, gave her a mock salute and went outside to join the party.

The afternoon was a welcome respite from the weeks of high-level stress. The men relaxed and unwound. Frisbees were tossed and frequently stolen by Rerun. Adam grilled his promised kebabs, along with burgers and hot dogs. Charlie made a tub of water balloons for tossing after dinner with Jeremy squirting the hose more on Charlie than in the balloons. Liz stretched out on a chaise longue and watched the fun. This was the best Labor Day she could remember. Maybe because it felt like family—and she was just starting to realize how much she missed belonging to one.

As the party wound down and people started to leave, Liz crossed the lawn to join Charlie, who was watching Jeremy on the swing set. Rerun was stretched out on the grass beside her, also paying attention to the youngster.

"Hi." Charlie shaded her eyes from the afternoon sun. "That went well. I think everyone had a good time."

Liz plopped down beside her. "I think so, too." She looked around. "I thought Adam was out here with you."

"He was. He slipped inside to take a phone call from the hospital in Poplar Bluff."

"The investigation is moving along. More slowly than

I'd hoped for but at least we still have some leads to follow up on. And taking a few hours of R & R today I think reenergized the team."

"I agree. And don't worry about it moving slow as long as it's moving forward. Remember the fable about the tortoise and the hare? We both know who won that race. Don't worry. It will all work out."

Liz shook her head and chuckled. "What's your secret? Do you have a secret recipe for eternal optimism that you take with your morning smoothie?"

Charlie laughed. "I get down every now and then."

"Really? I'd like to see that just once."

"Hey, now, that's not nice." Charlie poked her and laughed again. "Just because you walk around like you have the weight of the world on your shoulders doesn't mean you have to come to the party and pop my balloon."

Liz waved her hand in a halting motion. "I know. You're right. But you're always smiling or humming or laughing. I envy you. It must be nice to be so up and optimistic all the time."

"I wasn't always this content."

"No? What changed?"

"Adam came into my life."

Liz's heart clenched. So, her suspicions were right. There was more than a professional relationship between Charlie and Adam. What a fool she'd been to ever entertain the idea that Adam was on the up-and-up and that he still had feelings for her.

"Mind my asking how long the two of you have been an item?" Liz tried to make her voice sound like the question was mild curiosity and not pain-numbing need to know.

Charlie laughed harder. "We're not an item. He's my

boss…and a really good friend. He's best friends with my brother Bob. They went to college together. That's how I met Adam. Bob brought him home to the ranch for the summer of their freshman year. Adam's been in and out of our lives ever since. Mainly in. My two brothers and I train dogs for a variety of services. Guide dogs as companions for the blind, deaf, and now other disabilities." She nodded in Jeremy's direction. "Like autism.

"We also train dogs for the police, for search and rescue, and my brother Hank just started a pilot program working with the local prison system. Some of the prisoners help train the puppies. Adam and Bob are the masterminds behind the whole thing. We used to be just an ordinary Montana ranch back in the good old days."

"I don't understand. You said Adam…"

Charlie reached out and rubbed the scruff of Rerun's neck. "Adam and I have had hundreds of conversations over the years. He's helped me put things in perspective, start looking at what good I can find even in the midst of bad situations. He was instrumental in helping us start the dog-training program. It's impossible to stay a grump when you're surrounded by puppies offering you nothing but love."

Charlie's tone quieted and her eyes sobered. "And I will be forever grateful to Adam for introducing me to the One who loves us unconditionally. My life has never been the same. So, yes, I suppose I do have a secret recipe that I take with my morning smoothie. I start my day with private time with the Lord."

Adam? He hadn't been a Christian when she'd known him. What had happened to him when he left Country Corners? There were so many things she saw in this man that she hadn't seen in the boy he'd been. Compassion. Thoughtfulness. Kindness. As much as she'd thought she'd loved Adam back then when he was a typical high school jock and the world revolved around him, she didn't want to admit that she was starting to like this new and improved version of Adam Morgan—a lot.

Almost as though he sensed she was thinking about him, she felt his presence behind her just moments before she noticed his shadow stretch out in front of her on the grass.

"Penny for your thoughts."

Liz looked up at him and smiled. "Sneaky way to collect money, Dr. Morgan, charging people for their thoughts."

"Only certain people. Only the ones whose thoughts I want to hear."

"Okay, that's my cue to make myself scarce." Charlie chuckled, stood up and brushed fresh-cut grass off her jeans.

Liz bounced up. "You don't have to leave. I'm going inside. I have tons of work waiting for me."

"It's time to take Jeremy inside, anyway." Charlie signaled Rerun to rise.

Liz glanced at her watch to keep herself from having to look at Adam. She knew just one glance into those beautiful golden-brown eyes of his and she'd follow him as obediently as Rerun. "I have reports waiting for me. It was a great day today, Adam. Thank you so much for what you did for my team." Without a backward glance she hurried across the lawn to the house.

She was sitting at her desk reviewing the latest reports when she heard a bloodcurdling scream that chilled her to the bone. It was quickly followed by the earsplitting sound of the security alarm going off. She knocked over her chair and raced through the doorway of the study and into the foyer.

Jeremy screamed again at the top of his lungs. He ran in circles at jet-propelled speed around the middle of the foyer. Adam and Charlie, caught off guard by the child's sudden outburst and the ear-piercing security alarm, hesitated for a moment, and then they both joined the chaos. Charlie grabbed the boy as he raced past and subdued him. Adam ran toward the alarm box to punch in the code.

The front door stood wide open and a man, his mouth open in astonishment, stood in the doorway.

It took Liz only a second to comprehend what had happened. The man in the doorway wore a delivery-man's uniform. Jeremy was terrified of people in uniforms.

What was the door open for, anyway? What had they been thinking? No one was supposed to open doors in this house except one of her deputies or herself. What if it had been the killer? Maybe it was.

Liz sprinted past the group in the foyer, ushered the man back outside and pulled the door shut behind her.

"I'm so sorry. I didn't mean to scare the kid. I was just dropping off this package. The kid opened the door and started screaming." The deliveryman mopped his brow with a handkerchief and looked as if he was still trying to recover from what had happened.

One hand surreptitiously on the gun tucked at her side under her blouse, she glanced over his shoulder to the large van parked in the driveway and then back to the man on the stoop.

"Sorry about that. The boy is autistic and has a deep-seated fear of people in uniforms." Liz grimaced. "He's seen plenty of them recently so I'm surprised he reacted as violently as he did to you."

Liz did a quick inspection of the man's badge, matching picture to face and memorizing his name.

"Is he going to be okay?" The man shoved his handkerchief back in his pocket and picked up the package he had dropped on the step.

"He'll be fine. Here, let me take that from you."

The man couldn't dump the box in her arms fast enough, turned and almost ran to his truck.

Liz grabbed a notepad and stubby pencil from her back pocket and wrote down his name and the license plate. She called Darlene on her cell phone, gave her the information and asked her to check him out. He probably was nothing more than what he appeared to be but Liz wasn't taking any more chances with Jeremy's safety.

She quickly examined the package in her hands. The return address was a business in New York. The package was light. It didn't rattle when shook. She held it to her ear. If it was a bomb, it wasn't ticking. Still not wanting to take any unnecessary chances, she carried it a safe distance from the house, placed it under an evergreen tree and called Davenport to have one of his bomb-squad guys come out and take a look.

She hurried back into the house and her heart squeezed at the sight in front of her. The boy perched on the second step of the stairway, Charlie and Adam sitting on either side of him. Rerun kept trying to get to the boy but Charlie ordered him away.

Jeremy, hair wet with sweat, his eyes red from crying, grasping his teddy bear tightly to his chest, was taking deep, stuttering breaths. When he saw her he yelled, "Mommy. Jeremy wants Mommy. Jeremy wants Mommy."

Liz closed the door behind her and leaned against

it. She vowed to find the man who had destroyed this child's world—and she would make him pay.

He lowered himself into the closest seat and stared aimlessly out the window. He needed a plan. No more flying by the seat of his pants. No more reacting first and thinking about it later. He needed a solid, no-fail plan to get his hands on that kid and find out once and for all what he knew.

He drummed his fingers on the kitchen table.

He couldn't believe how lucky this kid was. Since when are kids quiet? But this one was. How else could he have seen what was going on between him and his parents that night and not be seen himself?

Yep. Quiet and sneaky.

Hiding in a closet under a pile of blankets in his mama's closet.

Unbelievable.

I guess his luck rubbed off on the sheriff, too. Who would have believed you could shoot out the tires of a car going at least fifty miles an hour, watch it fly through the air and land upside down in a ditch and then blow up—and have all three of them walk away with nothing more than nuisance injuries? It was like they were wearing some kind of invisible protective shield and nothing he did could kill them.

He rubbed his chin with his hand. A skittering across the table caught his peripheral vision. His hand shot out and slammed down on top of the cockroach. He wiped the remains on his pant leg.

That was just plain stupid thinking.

They didn't have any special protection. They were human beings just like everybody else. And human beings could be killed just like cockroaches. He just hadn't used the right roach spray yet.

He took two slabs of white bread, a slice of tomato, some mayo and threw three slices of turkey in the middle. He banged a pot on the stove, opened a can of soup, dumped it in and turned up the heat.

He was getting pretty sick of eating sandwiches and soup.

He grabbed the pot off the stove and dumped it into the sink. He was tired of stinkin' soup. He took a bite of his sandwich. It would have to do for tonight.

He didn't have much of an appetite, anyway. The cocaine made sure of that.

He'd been crazy to ever try the stuff in the first place.

But he'd been angry…and lonely…and maybe just a bit curious.

Now it was a chain around his neck, making him do things he'd never have believed he'd ever do. Making him do things that normally would have shamed him.

But not anymore.

As soon as he cleaned up this problem and he knew he was in the clear, he was going to start a new life. He was going to kick his habit. Never should have started it in the first place. Time for him to pack it in.

Maybe he'd move to another town. Maybe meet a woman who would appreciate him and settle down. Yeah, that's what he was going to do.

Just as soon as he figured out what to do about the kid.

NINE

Adam stood quietly in the bedroom doorway and simply watched.

Jeremy was sitting in the middle of the floor with a book open on his lap. Rerun's head was lying on the boy's legs. If dogs had expressions, Adam thought this one would definitely be anticipation. The crazy mutt looked like he expected Jeremy to start reading him the book any second now.

"How's he doing?" Liz's voice was a low whisper as she tiptoed up beside him.

"See for yourself." Adam gestured into the room. "Charlie's done a great job getting the two of them to bond. Rerun was quite instrumental in not only calming Jeremy earlier today after that deliveryman fiasco but he's actually got the boy talking."

"Talking?" Liz could barely conceal the excitement and surprise in her voice.

Adam held up his hand. "Whoa, calm down. It's nothing to get too excited about just yet."

"Well, what is he saying?" Liz asked in a louder whisper, and shifted her position for a better view into the room.

"Mostly gibberish. He stops talking if I get too close. But I definitely heard him tell Rerun about a 'bad man.'"

"'Bad man'? Do you think he's talking about the killer?"

"Maybe."

Liz's face twisted in concentration. When she spoke again, she sounded disappointed. "Maybe he's talking about the deliveryman."

Adam shrugged. "Hard to tell just yet. But it doesn't matter, anyway."

"Doesn't matter? Of course it matters. We need to know if Jeremy saw the man that killed his parents. We need to know if he has any other memories of that night that might help with our investigation."

"Shh." Adam gently pulled her out of the doorway and into the hall. "I know, but he has to open up on his own and in his own time."

"We're running out of time, Adam. I can't run my office from here indefinitely and I can't request federal marshal protection in WITSEC if I can't prove he was a witness. He'll end up in foster care and there will be no one to protect him." He heard the catch in her voice. "I can't let that happen to him."

"I understand. I do." He tilted her chin and looked into her shimmering blue eyes. Tendrils of her silken hair slid across his hand. The slight whiff of lilacs teased his nostrils and brought a smile to his face. He didn't expect a sheriff to wear perfume but on this one it seemed a perfect choice.

"These things can't be rushed, Liz. Both for the boy's mental health as well as for the integrity of your case. If we ask questions too soon or push too hard, the prosecution can say what we present was coerced or manufactured. They'll throw it out of court."

"I know." She reached up and cupped his wrist with her hand. "Thank you for what you are doing. You've helped Jeremy more than I ever thought anyone could."

Her touch sent every nerve ending in his body zinging. The blood pounded in his temples and his pulse quickened. He wanted to pull her into his arms and comfort her.

No, he didn't.

He wanted to pull her into his arms and kiss the living daylights out of her. Not the sweet adolescent kisses of their childhood, but the passionate, demanding kisses of adults. He wanted to taste the fullness of her lips. He wanted to slide his arm around her waist and pull her close. He was a full-grown man with normal physical reactions and, at this moment, that was all he could think about.

The silkiness of her hair. The beauty of her eyes. The scent of her skin.

Lizzie.

The only girl who had ever staked a solid claim to his heart.

The girl whose heart he had shattered into a million pieces.

That thought brought back the pain he'd felt the night he'd left town. How could he have been so stupid to believe he was the only one who would be hurt by his decision? Now he was certain his pain had been nothing compared to what she must have endured. At least he knew why he left. He had had time to process it, justify it. To her, he was just a louse who hadn't been man enough to say goodbye.

The memories doused his feelings as surely as if someone had thrown a bucket of ice water on his head. What made him think he deserved a second chance with

Lizzie? After the way he'd treated her, it was a miracle she bothered with him at all and he couldn't blame her. But if it was the last thing he did, he was going to prove to her that he was a decent man, a trustworthy man—and he knew he had to slow down and give her time and space to see it. Adam dropped his hand and stepped back. He tried not to read anything into the questioning look on her face.

"It's a good thing that Jeremy is starting to talk to Rerun," he said. "The boy has pent-up images and emotions bursting to get out. The dog makes him feel safe. It's only a matter of time before he says more—and says it louder than a whisper. When he does, one of us will be close by to hear it, too."

Liz nodded.

"Hey, you guys, I'm not interrupting anything, am I?" Charlie, holding a snack tray of apple slices and peanut butter, grinned so wide it looked too big for her face. "I don't know, Adam. Every time I leave you for a minute I catch you cozying up to our local sheriff. What's that about, huh?"

Heat crept up his neck. He reached out and ruffled her auburn hair. "That's about none of your business." He spun her toward the open doorway. "I think your services are needed elsewhere, young lady."

Charlie laughed out loud. "Okay. I'm going." She took a few steps into the room and then said over her shoulder in a singsong voice, "But I'm telling Bob."

Her childish behavior and laughter was contagious and both Adam and Liz laughed, too.

Adam turned his attention back to Liz and shook his head from side to side. "She's always been a little brat. Following Bob and me around. Spying on us. Little tattletale."

Liz chuckled. "Sounds like a perfect little sister to me."

Adam glanced at the woman in the room and back at Liz. "That she is. Couldn't love her more if she was my own flesh and blood. I'm going to miss her."

"Miss her?"

"C'mon, let's go downstairs and talk. Knowing Charlie, I'm sure she prepared a snack for us, too."

Adam cupped her elbow and led her to the stairs. He waited until they were seated at the kitchen counter enjoying a hot cup of coffee and a plate of homemade chocolate chip cookies before he picked up the thread of their conversation.

"Charlie's going to head home tomorrow afternoon. Rerun and Jeremy have bonded. It's a good match. Her work is over."

Adam studied her expression and thought he read genuine disappointment there.

"I'm sorry to hear that. I've enjoyed having her around."

"Me, too. But her brothers have been holding down the fort. They need her back."

Liz took a sip of her coffee. "She told me about the ranch…and the dogs…and that you started the whole thing."

Adam bit into a cookie and couldn't resist running his tongue along his lip to catch every chocolate morsel. "Not just me. It's a four-way partnership—my best friend, Bob; Charlie; their brother, Hank; and I. I fronted most of the start-up costs and offered my professional services for helping design the different guide programs for the specialized clientele. They've done all the work. I'm really proud of them. If everything continues on track, they should be able to buy me out by next fall.

The business is thriving and I fully expect them to develop national franchises soon."

"Wow, that's commendable, Adam. Who would have thought quarterback Adam Morgan would grow up to be not only an entrepreneur, but one whose product changes the lives of so many people?"

Adam wondered which product she referred to—the dog training, which she seemed to admire, or his psychiatrist services, which she was always vehemently against when they were younger. But now was not the time for that conversation.

He couldn't help feeling a glow of pride and he allowed himself to bask a little in her compliment. It felt good to hear Liz praise him, good that she could find some redeeming quality in him. It was more than he deserved but everything he wanted.

The conversation shifted to general, less personal topics like current events, the weather, local news. They finished off the cookies, downed enough coffee to keep them up half the night and just enjoyed each other's company.

It had been a long, long time since Adam had had such a relaxing evening and he didn't want it to end. He glanced at the clock. Her shift relief would be here in another hour and then she'd disappear into her room. But he still had that hour.

By mutual agreement, they moved into the study. Adam picked up the book he'd been trying to read. Liz crossed straight to her computer and checked her emails.

Both of them looked up as Charlie and Rerun bounded down the stairs. She poked her head in the study. "Jeremy's been asleep about an hour. I'm almost finished packing." She lifted her hand with the leash in it. "I'm going to take Rerun out back to do his business for the evening and then I'm turning in. I have a long drive tomorrow."

Liz swung her computer chair around to face her. "I'm sorry to see you go."

Adam seemed to have a walnut-size lump in his throat at the thought of Charlie leaving. He knew it would be too long until he saw her again and that lump was doing a good job of keeping him from being able to say anything at all.

"Now don't the two of you go all mushy on me. There'll be plenty of time in the morning for good-byes. I'm not heading out until I cook up one storm of a breakfast. Dream tonight of the hash browns, bacon, sausage, eggs and cinnamon buns that will be waiting for you in the morning."

"Cinnamon buns?" Liz laughed and patted her stomach. "I've already gained two pounds eating your cookies."

Charlie shot a grin at Liz. "Laughter sounds good on you. You should do it more often." She headed toward the kitchen.

They both heard the back door slam and went back to their business.

Minutes later, they heard Rerun barking furiously. It was the frantic tone of it that caught Liz's attention.

Adam rose to see what was going on and Liz followed. They reached the kitchen just as Rerun burst through the back door, straining on the leash so hard that Charlie had to let it go before she fell on her face.

"What the...?" Adam watched the dog bound for the stairs.

"I don't know." Charlie, out of breath from being pulled across the yard, righted herself from her almost prone position. "I've never seen him like this. He was sniffing around like he always does, then he alerted, sniffed the air and took off. I couldn't stop him. He wouldn't listen to me."

"Jeremy." Liz drew her weapon and raced for the stairs.

Adam and Charlie were close behind. When the three of them reached the loft, they saw Rerun scratching furiously at Jeremy's bedroom door. The dog would actually pause, jump up to throw his front paws against the wood and then scratch again.

Adam didn't know what was worse—the piercing sound of the security alarm when it had tripped earlier or the echoing frantic barking of a panicked dog.

"Something's wrong." Liz ran to the door. She yelled for Charlie to get hold of Rerun. Then she gestured for Adam and Charlie to move to the side and out of the line of possible fire.

Adam recognized the command in her eyes and knew she wouldn't appreciate his expression of concern or any interference. He clenched his teeth but moved aside, showing her the respect due her as the sheriff. He knew she was fully capable of handling whatever waited behind that door. But he would be one step behind her when she went in—just in case she needed him.

Once she seemed certain Charlie and Adam were safe, she slowly turned the doorknob, threw open the door and entered with gun drawn.

Adam saw her holster her weapon and run.

He ran after her.

She crouched over a crumpled bundle on the floor beneath the open window.

"Is he okay?" Charlie pushed her face over Adam's arm so she could get a closer look but he held her back and wouldn't let her get any closer.

"Give Liz a chance to check things out."

Liz lifted a rag from the floor, holding it gingerly between her index finger and thumb. She brought it to her face, took a whiff and looked at Adam.

"Chloroform."

"Chloroform?" Charlie grabbed a plastic bag of computer discs and emptied them on the desk. She held it out to Liz. "Put it in here."

Liz dropped the rag into the bag and sealed it up. It wasn't ideal—the forensic guys would have a cow— but the rag would only get more contaminated if she left it out.

Meanwhile, Adam checked Jeremy's pulse and his pupils and carried the child back to his bed. "Adam?" The fear in Liz's voice clenched at his heart.

"Is he alive?" Charlie asked.

Both women's faces wore worried expressions and Adam hurried to reassure them. "He's going to be fine."

Jeremy began to stir. He rubbed his fists against his eyes. When he opened them, he said, "Bad man. Jeremy said no. No bad man."

Liz's eyes watered and she smiled at the child. "You're right, Jeremy. No to the bad man. Good job."

This wasn't the first time in the past two weeks that Adam had witnessed this tender, maternal side of the normally tough, take-no-prisoners sheriff and, as much as he didn't want it to, it endeared her to him even more.

Liz, being careful not to touch the windowsill, leaned her head out the open window. Quickly she drew back inside and shouted at Charlie, "I just saw a man dressed in black dart into the trees. Call the station. Get help out here. Give them that description and make sure you tell them an officer is in pursuit."

"Wait a minute!" Adam's heart thundered in his

chest. It was one thing to let her enter a room first when he knew he was right behind her if she needed help. It was another to watch her run off into the night alone in pursuit of a killer. "What are you doing?"

When she looked at him, her gaze was hard, cold and determined.

"My job."

She drew her weapon and raced from the room.

Tree branches slapped her face and ground vines threatened to wrap around her feet and trip her. Although Liz had made concessions about not wearing a uniform around Jeremy, at this moment she was grateful that hadn't included her gun or her boots. She had to admit she wished she'd had her flashlight or her two-way radio right now, though.

She moved as quickly as possible through the thicket and brush and squinted her eyes for more focus in the darkness. Lit only by moonlight, it wasn't an easy trail to follow. The man was nothing more than a shadow among shadows—except he was the shadow that ran.

When she thought she'd lost him, she paused, stood perfectly still and listened.

Quite a distance ahead, to her left, it sounded like a herd of elephants crashing through the brush. Whoever this guy was, he didn't know the first thing about stealth. Now that she knew which direction to go, she too threw stealth to the wind and broke into a full-out run in an attempt to close the distance between them. She barely noticed the brambles biting through her pant legs or the sharp stinging of unforgiving branches as she rushed past.

Chest heaving, breath coming in deep gasps, Liz burst free from the woods and spilled onto the main road just in time to see the rear lights of a car disappear around the bend.

Whoever this guy was, he wasn't stupid. He'd taken a chance parking his vehicle on the main road where it could have been easily spotted or even hit. But he seemed to know the risk was minimal and that this stretch of road was barely used at this time of night. He knew better than to turn his headlights off and ease up the dirt road to the circular driveway. He'd rather carry a chloroformed child through the woods than chance being spotted during a perimeter check or by someone hearing tires crunch on gravel.

But why didn't he kill Jeremy when he'd had the chance? He could have easily smothered the child in his sleep or slit his throat or strangled him. Why kidnap him? He knew the parents weren't alive to pay ransom for the boy's return. He had made sure of that.

Liz's insides simmered with anger and a healthy dose of fear. This had happened on her watch. Right under her nose. She'd allowed herself to get complacent, too comfortable with Charlie, too on edge and aware of Adam. She had let down her guard. She never would have forgiven herself if anything had happened to Jeremy.

The welcome sound of sirens and the sight of flashing lights drew her attention as two cars spun into the sharp right leading to the house.

Liz jogged up to the dirt road. Her face felt as if it had been stung by a thousand bees and her thigh, still recovering from the auto accident, throbbed each time her foot hit the ground, but still she continued jogging until she reached the gravel driveway, and then she walked the rest of the way. As she approached, she saw Sal, Paul and Adam standing under the portico. Adam gestured wildly toward the woods. Probably insisting that they go looking for her. Paul was the first to see her.

"You okay, Sheriff?"

"I'm fine."

Paul shone a flashlight in her face as she approached and Liz had to reach up and shield her eyes.

"You don't look fine. You look like you should see a doctor."

"Paul, stop shining that light in my face."

As she stepped beneath the porch light, she heard a collective gasp.

Sal immediately crossed to her side. He stared hard at her face but otherwise showed no outward signs of emotion. It seemed neither one of them wanted an emotional repeat of the day of the accident. "So, who won? You or Muhammad Ali?"

Liz grinned and then grimaced as pain shot through her face.

"Did you catch him?" Adam asked.

"No, he had a car waiting on the main road. I got there just in time to get a good look at his taillights disappearing around a curve—but, unfortunately, not quick enough to catch any of the license plate numbers."

"I don't get it. Why'd he try to snatch the kid? Why didn't he just kill him?" Paul's puzzled expression echoed her feelings completely. "Maybe the guy drew the line on killing a kid."

"Then why snatch him?" Liz asked. "What was he going to do with him if not kill him?"

"This man didn't have any trouble brutally beating and killing the child's parents. It's not that far a leap for me to believe he intended to kill Jeremy as well," Sal said.

"Then why didn't he?" Liz's question hung in the air between them.

"We won't know until we catch him, will we?" Sal turned his attention to business. "What do you want us to do, boss?"

Grateful that Sal was there to help step in and run things, she said, "Do what you need to do, guys. Sal, call it in. The perp was dressed all in black and wore boots. His car was a four-door sedan. I think black, maybe dark green. Hard to tell in just moonlight. I only got a glimpse of it. I'm judging mostly from the size and shape of the trunk. When you're done, see if you can find any prints on the windowsill in Jeremy's bedroom or any other forensic evidence in the room.

"Paul, you catch up with Charlie. She has the chloroform rag in a bag. We need to get it to the lab, then you can give Sal a hand."

Gingerly she touched her eye. She could feel the swelling. She was going to have one prize-winning shiner in the morning.

"Tomorrow, when it's light, we'll take a closer look at those woods," she said. "Even though it's been dry as a bone these last few weeks, we could get lucky and find a boot print or two. You never know." She grinned and looked down at her torn jeans. "And with any kind of luck, maybe we'll find a piece of ripped clothing from him to help us."

The two men grabbed gear out of their cars and went to work.

As soon as they disappeared upstairs, Adam stepped forward and slid his arm around her shoulders. "Come with me, Sheriff. I have an ice bag with your name all over it."

"Hmm, handcuffs now ice. As long as you don't bring up the subject of whipped cream...."

Adam laughed and, pulling her closer, led her into the house.

Charlie looked up from her perch at the kitchen counter when they entered. "Wow! Tell me you beat the bad genes right out of that guy."

Liz laughed and then winced. "Sorry, Charlie. Never laid a hand on him. Never got close enough. I have some nasty tree branches to thank for this." She gestured to her face and collapsed on a nearby stool.

Charlie stepped closer. "Look at the size of that lip."

"Charlie."

A stern admonishment from Adam wasn't enough to silence her. "I'd be careful and stay away from Rerun for a little while. He absolutely loves sausage."

"Charlie!"

"What? I'm just saying."

"We could use ice. Lots of it."

Charlie tilted her head and took a hard look at Liz's face. "You need more than ice." She threw a look over her shoulder at Adam. "You get the ice. I'll grab the first-aid kit." She hurried from the room.

"Sorry about that." Adam wrapped ice in a dish towel and gingerly held the pack against the side of her face. "Charlie's never been known for her tact."

Liz started to smile but remembered what happened when she moved that bottom lip and instantly stopped. She took the ice pack from Adam's hand and held it against her lip.

Adam moved to the sink. When he returned, he carried a warm, wet cloth and washed her face, moving the cloth in slow, gentle circles against her skin. The task was strictly professional—a doctor tending to the wounds of the injured. But the painstakingly gentle way he touched her, the feel of his breath fanning her skin, the warmth emanating from the nearness of his body. It seemed so intimate, so personal, she could barely breathe.

"You scared me, you know." His voice had a deep, husky tone.

"Scared you?"

"Running off into the dark…alone…after a suspected killer."

"It's what I do. I'm the sheriff, Adam…and sometimes the job is dangerous."

"I know." His eyes darkened in intensity. "But it was hard watching you go. I was worried."

She reached up and caught his wrist before he could finish his task.

"Why would you worry?"

"We may not be together anymore but we're still friends."

"'Friends'?" She directed a steady, probing gaze at him. "Is that what we are, Adam? Friends?"

"The two of you can figure all that out later." Charlie burst into the room with her usual bolt of energy and nudged Adam away with her hip. "Right now, we're working together to fix up the sheriff's face. Then the three of us are going to figure out what happened here tonight and how we are going to make sure it doesn't happen again."

Charlie smeared first-aid cream on a cut on Liz's cheek and then ministered to the cuts on her hands, which she'd used to shield her face.

"I thought you were leaving in the morning." Adam perched on the edge of a counter stool.

"I can't leave now. It's getting too exciting around

here." She capped the antiseptic cream and tore the wrappers off a couple of Band-Aids. "Besides, you guys need me."

Adam grinned. "Thanks, Charlie. I didn't want to ask because I know how much you want to get home. But if you could stay a few more days…"

"Oh, I'm staying." She reached over and poked an index finger against Adam's chest. "And wait until you get my bill. I'm charging you double time for pain and suffering."

Liz tried not to laugh out loud at the shocked expression on Adam's face.

"What pain and suffering?"

"The pain and suffering I know is coming down the pike if the three of us don't come up with a better plan than what we've been doing. That guy got into the house with all three of us here and we didn't even know it. He knew our routine. He knew I'd turn the security system off when I walked Rerun. He was watching and waiting. If it hadn't been for Rerun, we wouldn't have known until it was too late."

That thought sobered Liz instantly. "Speaking of Rerun, where is he? And how is Jeremy?"

"Jeremy's fine. He's asleep in your bed and Rerun is spread out on top of him." Charlie smiled at her. "I think you'll be more comfortable if you sleep somewhere else tonight. I'm willing to share my room."

"Thanks for the offer but I don't expect to be getting much sleep tonight. I think I'll bunk on the couch."

"No, you won't."

Both women threw a questioning glance Adam's way.

"We're packing up and moving out. Right now."

TEN

"Where are we going?" Charlie sat down next to Adam.

"We're moving to a safe house. And we have to do it quickly before that nutcase comes back here in time to follow us to our new location or, worse, tries something else."

"What are you talking about? We're not going anywhere." Liz rose, planted her hands on her hips and glared at him. "You're the one who insisted that we move back here. You said it was important for Jeremy's mental health to return to the scene of the crime. We've been here five days and now you think you're going to uproot him again. I don't think so."

Adam ran a hand through his hair and sighed. "Look, Liz. It's the only safe and rational thing to do. Charlie's right. There were three adults in this house and, still, he got into Jeremy's room unobserved. We might not be so lucky next time."

"So, what do you have in mind? If you want me to get Jeremy placed in the witness protection program, I'm going to need some time to make the arrangements. We can't just pack up, knock on a federal marshal's door, and say, 'Here we are.'"

Liz chewed on her lower lip. Ouch. What a lousy way to break a habit, but maybe this swollen lip would turn out to be a good thing after all. She looked at Adam again.

"Will Jeremy be okay emotionally if we move him this quickly?" She searched his face, looking for assurances she knew he couldn't give in his expression. "I thought you said he needed to be in familiar surroundings to heal. Were you wrong?"

Adam ignored her underlying question. "I wasn't wrong, Liz. Since communication is such a difficult thing for Jeremy, it was important for him to return to his home, sleep in his own bed, and slowly start to realize his parents weren't here and weren't going to be. Ideally, I would have liked to stay here for another few weeks. But Jeremy's safety has become top priority.

"Familiarity will be the key to a successful transition. Now that Charlie's staying on a few more days, that will help, too. We'll keep the same people around him. Bring his things. His computer. His bear. Stick as close as possible to his daily schedule. Rerun will do the rest."

Charlie stood. "While you two are ironing out the particulars, I'm going to start packing Jeremy's things."

They watched her leave and then Liz turned her attention back to Adam.

"We can't just pick up in the middle of the night and disappear."

"Why not?"

"For a thousand reasons. Do you realize how difficult it was to get a remote office set up here? My team, not to mention Davenport and his men, will have a fit if I switch locations again."

"You won't be. You'll move back to your office in town and conduct business as usual."

"That's impossible. I won't be able to protect Jeremy from town."

"You weren't able to protect Jeremy here."

His words hit her with the force of a physical blow. He was right. She'd failed. Big-time.

"You didn't do anything wrong, Lizzie." He spoke as if he could read her mind. "None of us did. But the killer knows this house, its layout. He knew exactly where Jeremy would be and how to gain access to him.

"The killer didn't get all of that from one time inside when he was committing homicide. He's been back. He must have been sitting in those woods and watching us for days because he knew our routine. We only turn the security alarm off twice each evening, once when Charlie takes Rerun out for his final run and, again, when your relief shows up and you do the final perimeter walk. He made his move during one of those times."

Liz digested this information and had to agree with his take on things.

"So, what do you have in mind?"

"I bought a property on the outskirts of town, a large six-bedroom home sitting on ten acres of farmland."

"The old Granger estate?"

Adam nodded.

"No one's lived there for years."

"Exactly. That's why it's the perfect place to hide. I rented a room from old Mrs. Willowby over her general store when I moved back to town so I'd have a place to stay while I did some renovations out there. I haven't spoken about the project to anyone. There's no reason for anyone to tie me to the property. Since it's been empty for years, I doubt whether anyone will have any reason to think about looking out there, either."

Liz started to see the wisdom of his proposal. It just might work.

"I'll go upstairs and tell the men. They can help us with the move."

"No." Adam placed a hand on her arm. "You can't tell anyone, Liz. Not one single word. We have to just disappear. Period. It's the only way I can be sure that we will be safe."

"But I have to tell my team—"

"No one, Liz. That would be a deal breaker. This whole idea hinges on secrecy."

"I can't protect Jeremy by myself, Adam, particularly if I'm going back to work in town. I need my team and Davenport's men to help."

"We won't need protection if nobody knows where we are."

"You can't be sure of that."

"Think about it, Liz. If only three people know where Jeremy is—and those three people are one hundred per cent invested in saving Jeremy's life—then I think that is the safest situation you can get. Three people. You. Charlie. Me. What can go wrong? Can you guarantee me anything safer than that?"

"What about the killer? You didn't put him in the equation."

"Yes, I did. He was here tonight. He tried to snatch Jeremy. You chased him on foot and he took off in a car. At this moment, we know he's not here watching. We can be pretty sure he'll come back. But if we move now, right now, he won't be able to watch or follow. He'll have no idea where we are."

Liz wasn't comfortable with this idea. But the more she listened to Adam, the more it made sense. There was no reason for anyone to connect Adam to the old

Granger estate. They'd be safer there than anywhere else she could think of at the moment. And if she could return to town, she'd be able to assist more with the ongoing investigations. Maybe they could speed things up and end this nightmare sooner. It was unorthodox. Sure. But she was the sheriff and she made the rules. Heaven help her, but it was starting to sound like a feasible plan.

Adam dropped his hold on her arm. "If we're going to do this, we have to move fast. You have to get rid of Sal and Paul. Now. They can't know we're leaving."

She shot a troubled glance Adam's way. He was asking her to make a split-second decision. And it wasn't a simple decision, like what vegetable should they have for dinner? This was a drastic step. Not one she would normally even consider. Whatever choice she made would have long-lasting effects on a small boy's life.

Liz turned the idea over and over in her mind. She had always run things by the book, followed the rules just like her father had taught her. No one would ever expect her to sanction this idea—and that might be the very reason it could work.

Adam's eyes locked with hers in an intense, steady stare. "Trust me."

Trust him?

Dear Lord, I trusted him once with my heart and he shattered it into a million pieces. Do I dare trust him again—this time with my life and the life of that innocent child? Help me make the right decision, Lord.

Liz closed her eyes and took a minute to be still and think. When she opened them again, she knew they were filled with an optimism she hadn't felt in a long time. She looked at Adam and nodded. "Let's do it."

* * *

Back at the station, Liz sat at the head of the conference table and watched the members of the investigation team take their places "Thank you, everyone, for being so flexible with all the changes that I've thrown your way in the past two weeks. Hopefully, this should be the last of them."

"So, what's going on, boss?" Sal asked.

"Dr. Morgan and Jeremy have left town so I will be assuming my duties here."

A murmur of voices traveled the table.

"Define 'left town'?" Davenport asked.

"Just what I said. They're gone. We don't have to worry about protecting them anymore." She turned her attention to the sergeant. "I want to thank you and your men, Frank, for the extra watch details. I appreciate all your efforts, but we won't be needing your men anymore."

"Where did they go, Sheriff? Everybody was there plain as day last night." Paul shot her a puzzled look.

"Their whereabouts are unimportant. They're safe. What matters now is this investigation."

"You can't be serious." Sal looked troubled. "You're not going to tell us where Morgan took the kid? How do you know you can trust him?"

"I just know."

"Why? Because he proved to be so trustworthy in the past?"

Liz flinched at his words. Of course, it made sense that Sal would have snooped around in Adam's background. He would have wanted to know the connection between his sheriff and the new doctor in town.

"Jeremy is still a patient in Dr. Morgan's care. He has accepted full responsibility for Jeremy's welfare.

That's good enough for me." Liz flipped open the folder in front of her, shifted through some papers and moved one to the top. "Frank, what were the lab results?"

Davenport took her cue to drop the subject of the boy's location. "The toxicology report showed no sign of drugs. Autopsy results showed no track marks or physical evidence of prior drug use, either."

Liz nodded and moved on.

"Darlene, any luck with the video surveillance tapes?"

"No, Sheriff. Neither of them showed up on any of the tapes."

"Well, a sizable bag of cocaine doesn't hide itself under a bedroom mattress. There has to be a connection somewhere and we need to find it," Liz said.

"I thought Henderson might be selling coke, but that didn't pan out." Sal flipped through his own file folder. "I took a look at their financials. No unexplained deposits. Some debt but nothing out of the norm."

"Darlene and I took a look at Mr. Henderson's company books." Paul spoke for both of them. "His business was in the black and profits were steadily climbing."

"Well, the books might not be cooked, but there were a couple of little bumps within the business," Tom said.

All eyes turned his way.

"Henderson's only been in business since January and he's already fired two employees. Chad Richards was caught red-handed dipping into the petty cash box. I looked him up. He moved out of town right after the incident. Left a line of bill collectors in his wake. Doubt he'll show his face in this town anytime soon."

"Good job, Tom. And the other man?" Liz asked, taking notes as he spoke.

"That would be Eddie Simms. He's worth a second

look. Seems the guy has an anger management problem. Mouthed off one too many times with customers and Henderson let him go.

"Now, here's where it gets interesting. Eddie Simms is a gun nut. I followed up and ran a check on gun permits. Even hit a pawn shop or two in town about recent sales and had me some pretty interesting conversations. Eddie owns a cabin down by the lake filled with enough fire power to supply a small army. His weapon of choice—a high-powered rifle."

Tension in the room increased with this new information.

"Good going, Miller. Other than the wife beater, who I still think is a good candidate for last week's sniper attack, even if you don't," Sal said, throwing a telling glance at Liz, "I'd say this guy just became person of interest number two. Maybe he likes hunting patrol cars in his spare time."

Liz turned her attention to Sal. "Progress report on the dealer murder?"

"The security camera behind Smitty's bar was destroyed right about the time of the murder."

"Coincidental, wouldn't you say?" Davenport shifted in his chair. "Let me guess. Nothing useful on the film."

"You'd win that bet." Sal doodled on the outside of a file folder. "Smitty taped over that night before I could get to him."

"Sorry to hear that. Better luck next time." Davenport glanced at his watch and stood. "Have to run. Call me if you need anything else, Sheriff. Good luck with the investigation."

"Thanks, Frank, for all your help." Liz stood and shook his hand.

Once he was gone, she focused her attention back to her team.

"Okay. We have two suspects with high-powered rifles, good motives, but nothing to tie either one of them to any of the crimes. We have no suspects. No witnesses. No connection between our dead drug dealer and the Hendersons. Which still doesn't explain the cocaine we found hidden beneath Henderson's mattress."

Liz sighed heavily and looked at Sal. "But you think you might have a lead?"

"Might, boss. But nothing solid enough to share yet."

"Keep me in the loop." She took a swig of her coffee. "Tom, I want you to take another run at Grimes and that bank teller he's sleeping with. I want to know the real reason Grimes and Henderson fought. And attack their alibis. I want more than them stating they were with each other."

"I'm on it, Sheriff."

Liz stood and braced her fists on the table. "Jeremy saw what happened that night. I'd stake my badge on it. The good news is he's starting to talk. It's only a matter of time before he says something we can use."

"He is? That's terrific, Sheriff." Darlene clapped her hands together. "That little boy is such a doll. I'm so happy he's starting to get better."

"If he says anything, will it hold up in court?" Sal asked.

"I thought you said these kind of kids can't talk," Tom said.

Liz raised her hand in a halting motion. "I'll worry about the information standing up in court after I find out who the bad guy is, Sal. Yes, Darlene, it is wonderful that the boy is beginning to recover from that horrible night. And yes, Tom, this boy can not only talk but

I, for one, plan to listen when he does." Liz made eye contact with each one of them. "Meanwhile, it's just the five of us. Our team standing between a small boy and death. Let's get back out there and find us a bad guy."

He opened the front door and threw his keys in the glass bowl on the credenza. He kicked off his boots and left them at the front door. Then he walked through the master bedroom and straight into the bathroom. He removed the bandage from his side, lifted his shirt and studied his body in the wall-to-wall mirror over the double sinks.

The puncture wound was ugly, deep and red. It had taken him almost an hour to get it to stop bleeding. He'd had to pack the thing with gauze and tape it tight. He took the gauze out and winced at the pain. Tenderly he touched the edges of the wound. The surrounding skin was mottled, swollen and sore to the touch. He slathered more antiseptic cream on the area and placed clean gauze across the site.

He'd been lucky last night. His face mask and thick gloves had protected him from getting more than a sting or two from those tree branches as he raced through the woods. He hadn't expected the sheriff to catch him in the act and give chase. She was surprisingly fast moving through the dark woods with nothing more than moonlight to light her way. At least he'd had a small flashlight helping him see the path at his feet. She'd almost caught up with him, too. He couldn't afford to take another chance like that one.

He taped the gauze in place, lowered his shirt and took a good, hard look at the reflection staring back at him. His eyes were puffy. His cheeks had retracted and he was starting to look a bit gaunt. Wonder if anybody noticed. If they did, maybe they'd just think he was getting sick or something.

He washed a hand over his face.

When was this all going to end? How in the world had he let it start? If he could turn back time, he'd never have touched those drugs in the first place. What had he been thinking?

He hadn't. He'd been reacting to his feelings. He'd been in pain…and lonely…and angry. The opportunity to escape, to forget for just a little while, presented itself. And then everything mushroomed out of control.

He'd been doing good last night. He'd almost cleared the woods, skirting his way through the brush like a pro. Until he lost his balance and that one lone, stupid stick jabbed right into his side. It hurt like the dickens, too.

But not as much as the sheriff's face must be hurting. He saw her going into the police station this morning and he almost doubled over laughing when he got a look at that shiner and swollen lip. That would teach her. Stupid woman.

He'd made a really dumb mistake last night. He should have just killed the boy when he'd had the chance. But he wasn't sure that the boy had seen him that night. He didn't want another death on his conscience, particularly a kid's, unless he had no choice. He'd never intended to kill anyone in the first place.

He figured he'd snatch the kid and find out what he knew. If the boy recognized him, he'd get rid of him. If he didn't recognize him, he'd drop the kid in front of a hospital or firehouse or something.

Look how disastrous that turned out.

He'd slipped back to the house at first light only to find the place empty and everyone gone. Now he didn't have a clue where they went.

No more listening to that nagging voice of conscience in his hcad.

He was out of patience…and time. Not knowing if this kid could identify him was eating him up inside. Making him make bad choices. Do stupid things. There was no question anymore. He knew what he had to do. He had to find the kid…and this time he'd kill him.

ELEVEN

Liz checked her rearview mirror for the tenth time in the past five minutes. No one was following her. She'd been super careful. She wasn't even driving her own car. She'd borrowed Gus Crater's pickup truck. She told him she got the deal of a lifetime on a china cabinet at a garage sale near Poplar Bluff and she needed something bigger than her car or cruiser to haul it home.

The pea-green, rusted-out relic didn't have a shock absorber left in its body and Liz considered it almost a miracle that it still ran. But Gus loved his truck and he hadn't parted with it lightly. She'd not only had to promise to return it in the morning with a full tank of gas but she'd had to throw in prime seats to this weekend's basketball game. Gus drove a hard bargain.

Taking one more look behind her, she felt safe enough to head for the old Granger estate and turned the truck in that direction.

It took at least ten minutes for the piece of junk she was driving to make it across the ten acres of property. Liz was becoming a pro at driving down old unlit dirt roads with nothing more than moonlight and car headlights to guide her. But this time when the truck lights hit the house, it stole Liz's breath away.

The Victorian-style home had been deserted for years. There hadn't been any heirs to the estate and in this economy there weren't many millionaires buying homes in Country Corners. The years had taken a toll. The outside was weathered and forlorn looking. But it screamed with potential.

She could picture white wicker rocking chairs and fern baskets all along the wraparound porch. Potted geraniums hanging from the portico. Fresh paint and some minor repairs and this home could easily be restored to its original grandeur in no time.

Liz couldn't believe that Adam had purchased this property. What would a single man want with a house so large? Unless he wasn't intending to stay single for long. The thought brought a rush of heat to her face.

She turned off the ignition and stepped from the cab.

"Stop right there." Liz heard the distinctive sound of a shotgun being cocked behind her.

"I'd listen to him if I were you." The female voice had circled around and was coming at her from the front. "Put your hands above your head and do it now."

Liz immediately did as she was told.

"Adam? Charlie?"

"Liz?"

They were by her side in seconds. Adam shone a flashlight over her and then over the truck. "What the...? Where'd you get this piece of junk?"

"It runs and no one would be expecting me to be behind the wheel so I felt safer driving it out here than my patrol car or personal vehicle."

"Good idea." Charlie shone a flashlight on the ground by their feet. "Let's get in the house. It's spooky out here in the dark."

Once inside, Charlie excused herself and went upstairs to check on Jeremy and Rerun.

Adam led Liz past a living room decorated with upholstered sofas and comfortable armchairs. A large stone fireplace and hand-carved mantel was the focal point of the room.

Surreptitiously, he watched her, gauging her reaction, hoping to see approval in her eyes.

He led her through French doors into the solarium. The arched glass overlooked illuminated walking paths, hanging lanterns, benches, flowers and even a pond with a fountain. He didn't realize he'd been holding his breath waiting for her reaction until she spoke.

"Oh, Adam, this is stunning."

"I hoped you would like it." He clasped her elbow and a jolt of electricity ran through him just by touching her. He led her to a nearby chair. Once she was seated, he perched on the arm of the opposite chair and tried to mask this explosion of attraction he felt whenever he was with her. "How'd it go with your team? Anybody give you a hard time about not telling them where we are?"

"They weren't happy about it but no one made waves." Liz took a moment and looked around the room, "This place really is beautiful, Adam. But I must admit that I'm surprised you bought it."

"Remember I told you a few weeks ago that I had a special project that I would be working on for Country Corners?"

Liz nodded.

"Well, this is it. I'm giving this place a facelift and I'm turning it into a place for teenagers at risk. You know, kids on the fringe of making life-altering mistakes, where intervention from the right person at the right time might make all the difference."

He watched the blood drain from her face. She knew they'd have to have this conversation sooner or later.

"'Kids at risk'?" Her voice wavered but he pretended not to notice.

"Yes. Abused kids that need a safe place to stay for a while. Kids mixed up with the wrong crowd. Trying to get to them before they start experimenting with drugs. Kids on the fringe of escalating from minor juvenile offenses to serious crimes." He paused for a moment and then he said, "And emotionally needy kids. The kind that don't believe there's a place in this world for them. The suicidal kids."

Liz drew in a sharp breath. Speechless, she just stared at him.

"I'm calling it 'Luke's House.'"

Liz stared hard at him before she spoke. She stood and began to pace. "Your father was responsible for my brother's death. Now you come back to town and think if you build a teen center in his name that that will make everything okay?"

"Of course it won't."

"It didn't end with Luke's suicide either, did it? We had to live in that house with the memories and the guilt. It felt like the house was haunted. Luke was everywhere…and nowhere."

Adam didn't move. He didn't try to touch her. He just sat quietly and looked at her with empathy and compassion.

"The first few months after Luke's death, all my parents ever did was fight, constantly blaming each other. I didn't think it would ever end. But it did end. And the silence was worse. Three people living in a mausoleum.

It was torture. And then it was over. My mother took off. She kept in contact with me at first." Liz shrugged. "But I suppose as time went on she found it easier to make a clean break from everything." Her eyes glistened when she looked at him. "From me. I guess I'm collateral damage from an emotional explosion neither one of them ever recovered from."

Her pacing slowed and she came to a stop in front of him. "My father threw himself into his work. And me— We both know what happened to me, don't we, Adam?"

A muscle twitched in his jaw.

"I'm glad we're having this conversation, Lizzie. It's long overdue." He waited a moment and then he gestured to the chair. "Please, sit down. We need to talk."

Every muscle in her body appeared taut and tight like a deer startled in headlights wanting to run but frozen with fear. Precious seconds clicked by. This was it…the moment of truth…the chance to lay it all on the line and confess his failings and beg her forgiveness. If she'd just stay still long enough to listen.

Without saying a word, she slid back down to the chair opposite him.

"Lizzie." His voice softened and carried a great sorrow. He took a deep breath."My father didn't kill Luke. Luke killed himself."

Before she could verbally explode, he raised his hand in a halting motion. "My father did everything in his power to help your brother. But one-hour sessions twice a week weren't enough to cure the damage of living with a controlling, mean bully…and that's what your father was. He ridiculed Luke every day of his life. Why? Because Luke was artistic and creative. He was kindhearted and sensitive.

"Luke felt helpless against the big, strong sheriff of

Country Corners. Your father pushed and pushed until a teenage boy who had no coping skills and no spiritual foundation felt he had no other option."

Tears washed her cheeks and blurred her vision. "Stop it."

"You know it's true. Your mother knew it, too, but couldn't stop him. That's why your family fell apart after Luke committed suicide. It wasn't because of anything my father did or didn't do. It was because your family didn't have a strong spiritual foundation to help them through the troubled times. When the storms came the marriage crumbled."

He leaned forward and laced his fingers together. "And what happened to you, Lizzie?" He thought his heart would break but he forced himself to say what was in his heart. "You became another victim. The leftover child who did everything in her power to win her father's love, even followed in his footsteps to please him, so that she didn't have to follow in Luke's."

"Stop it!" She covered her ears with her hands. "I can't listen to this garbage anymore."

Adam fell on one knee in front of her and gathered her into his arms.

"No!" She pummeled his chest but he just embraced her more. "Don't touch me." She hit him again but this time her jabs lacked any significant force. Then she grasped the front of his shirt and buried her face in his chest and sobbed until he didn't think she had even one tear left.

"I remember it all. The raging fights between my father and Luke. The beatings. The tears. The fear. I loved my father—but I saw what he did to Luke and I feared him, too."

The self-recrimination and pain etched on her face

tore at his heart. None of his professional skills were helping him now. It was just the two of them...Lizzie and him...lost in the past...buried in pain and guilt and grief...with no way to climb into the present.

"Why couldn't your father help him?" Her eyes pleaded with him to help her understand. "Luke needed someone to help him."

"I know, Lizzie. I'm so sorry. Dad tried to help. He did. But one-hour sessions twice a week weren't enough. Not when Luke still had to go home each night to your dad. Sometimes kids need safe harbors, a sort of time-out for both the troubled teen and their families until they can get help and start to heal. That's what I want Luke's House to be."

"I loved Luke so much...and when I found him... lying across his bed...his eyes open...sightless."

"It's okay. Let it out. You've been holding it inside for way too long." Adam tilted her chin and looked into her eyes. "Bundle that pain up and give it to the Lord. Let Him carry it for you, Lizzie. He's been waiting for you to turn to Him for a very long time. Now just might be that time."

"I've always believed in the Lord, Adam."

"I know. You believed in Him long before I found my way to Him. But you've kept Him at a distance— at arm's length while you tried to find your own way through the storm." He smiled at her and brushed a strand of hair from her face. "From everything I've read in the Bible, God's pretty good when it comes to handling storms."

She smiled tentatively at him and it melted his heart. He pressed his lips against her forehead. He smoothed her hair off her face. "Lizzie..." He lowered his mouth and captured her lips as tenderly and lovingly as he could and he tasted the saltiness of her tears.

There was so much more to say. So many unanswered questions still hanging in the air between them but he didn't want to overwhelm her. She'd suffered enough tonight. With a gentle smile he released her.

"I'm going to turn in. I've prepared one of the spare bedrooms at the top of the stairs. Charlie's room is on the right. I've put you on the left of the staircase. Good night, Liz. See you in the morning."

He had crossed the room before she found her voice and called his name. He paused in the doorway.

"Why, Adam? Why did you leave me when I needed you most?"

He faced her with as much honesty as he could muster. "Because I was young…and stupid…and maybe a little afraid."

She arched an eyebrow. "Afraid? Of what?"

He searched her eyes to see if she was strong enough to take the blow he knew his answer would deliver. The steady, direct gaze she returned convinced him that Lizzie had grown in a thousand ways over the years. This wasn't a fragile teenage girl waiting for answers. It was a strong, independent, breathtakingly beautiful woman—and there could be no more secrets between them.

Liz's eyes never left Adam's face as he took a step back into the room. She could tell from his body language that he didn't want to answer her question but he would.

"After Luke's death, your father sent for me. He set up a meeting in the sheriff's office. Pretty intimidating for a teenage boy to be staring at a prison cell while your dad leaned back in his car, rested his hand on his gun and delivered news that changed my life."

Her father had sent for Adam. Why?

Her world had just been knocked off its axis. "What did he say?"

"He said you asked him to talk to me. You wanted me to stay away from you, that none of your family wanted anything to do with me or any of my family ever again."

"You believed him?" Her pulse beat an angry rhythm against the soft sensitive spots beside her eyes. How could her father have done that to Adam? To her?

"I was two days shy of my eighteenth birthday, Lizzie. I was a stupid kid. I didn't know what to believe. I told him I wanted to hear it from you. He said if I cared about you, then I wouldn't make things harder on you and I'd just go. He said that you had suffered enough after Luke died and the sight of me, or any of my family, would only cause you pain. He said you hated me."

Adam shook his head and his voice was heavy with sadness.

"I remember it all, Lizzie. The telephone calls I made to your house that were either intercepted or not answered. The pain I felt because I believed that you didn't want to be with me. The fear of your father and what he could do to me and to my family. When he told me he was seriously thinking of bringing my dad up on malpractice charges, I was scared. He promised to drop them if I'd leave town and never contact you again— that cinched the deal.

"I left for college and I never looked back. I never told my dad what happened, though he asked repeatedly why we broke up and why I was so insistent on leaving town so quickly." He locked his gaze with hers. "I honestly believed I was doing it for you. It took a long time for me to be honest with myself. After I found my faith, I was finally able to face the truth about myself. The Lord helped me see my mistakes...my sins...my flaws. And He loved me through them. I became a better man." He looked at her and raw, painful emotion was written on his face. "I left because I was afraid. I should have stayed and fought for you. Maybe I should have tried to take you with me. But I didn't. I ran."

He closed the distance between them. "You were right about me." Gently he pulled her into his embrace. "I was a coward...and I've regretted it a million times since...." He kissed her lips so softly it felt like the brush of butterfly wings. "But I'm here now, Lizzie. And I'm not a scared boy anymore. I'm a man...wanting to try to make amends...hoping for forgiveness...and maybe a second chance." When he lowered his head this time, there was nothing chaste or gentle about his kiss. It was an adult kiss filled with passion and longing and promises of a future that neither one of them had dreamt could ever be.

And she kissed him back...just as passionately... clinging to his waist...stepping into his embrace.

When he released her, he smiled into her eyes. "I love you, Lizzie. I always have."

Without another word, he turned and went upstairs.

Liz's world was reeling. Her father had threatened Adam? She knew what that looked like. She had seen him turn that ugly side of himself on Luke too many times. Bile rose in her throat and almost choked her.

Why hadn't she told someone what was happening in her house? Why hadn't she tried to help Luke? When she'd seen her father go after him, why had she run and hid? Why hadn't she intervened?

Guilt washed over her like a burning acid.

She'd always tried to please her father...always

searching for his love…even followed in his footsteps as sheriff, trying to be the son Luke couldn't be. But nothing she had ever done had been good enough and she had never known a father's love.

A voice inside her mind spoke to her. It wasn't true. She was precious and cherished in her heavenly Father's eyes. Adam was right. The Lord had been calling to her and waiting for her to turn over her life and heart and pain to Him for a very long time.

Liz fell to her knees and began to pray.

The next morning, Liz reached the bottom stair just in time to hear Charlie's voice outside.

"Rerun, no! Rerun, stop!"

Liz stepped onto the porch, shielded her eyes against the sun's glare and watched as Charlie sprinted across the lawn and grabbed the dog by the collar. "Let go."

The dog dropped the teddy bear that he had been trying to shred.

Charlie handed the bear back to Jeremy. "Sorry, Jeremy. He must have wanted to play with it, too." She turned to the dog and signaled. "Lie down."

Rerun did as she commanded and put his head on his paws but never took his eyes off the bear.

"I don't know what's gotten into him." Charlie joined her on the porch. "That's the second time in the past twenty-four hours that I've had to rescue that bear from Rerun's jaws. The dog wants to tear the thing to shreds. I don't get it. He didn't act that way before and it's not like his other toys that squeak when he bites them."

"Don't know what to tell you, Charlie. I guess that's why they pay you the big bucks to be the dog whisperer and not me." Liz chuckled and patted Charlie on the shoulder in a reassuring gesture.

"Have you seen Adam this morning?" Liz held her breath while she waited for the answer. How was she going to face him after what he'd told her last night? She'd blamed Adam and his family for every terrible, horrible thing that had happened to her family. She'd believed it was his father's lack of professional skills that caused her brother's suicide. She'd blamed living in the house where Luke had committed suicide as the eventual reason for her parents' divorce. She'd blamed Adam for leaving when she needed him most.

But none of it was true.

It was her father.

Her father had bullied Luke until he took his own life. Her father had bullied her mother until she was broken and so afraid that when she ran, she ran alone, leaving her behind. It was her father who had hated the Morgans so much that he'd lied to Adam and sent him away. The father she loved…and hated.

Her father.

How would she ever be able to face Adam again? Would he be able to forgive her? Would she be able to gather the courage to ask for that forgiveness?

"I haven't seen him yet." Charlie tossed a ball onto the lawn and both Rerun and Jeremy ran after it. "When I passed by his bedroom door, I thought I heard his shower running. I'm sure he'll be down in a little bit." She glanced over her shoulder and caught Liz's gaze. "So, how did it go last night?"

"How did what go?"

"Don't play coy." Charlie's perpetual grin was plastered on her face. "I left you alone so the two of you could talk."

"About what?"

Charlie placed her hands on her hips and for the first time since she'd met her, the woman frowned.

"I don't know what happened between the two of you years ago. But I do know this. Both of you still have feelings for each other. Whenever the two of you are in the same room together, the air zings with energy and awareness."

"Charlie, has anyone ever told you that you have an overactive imagination?"

"Stop fighting it! In case you haven't noticed, neither of you are kids anymore. It's time to settle the past and put it where it belongs—in the past. Think of all the wonderful possibilities for the future. So, did you talk last night or did I confine myself to my room for nothing?"

Heat rushed up Liz's throat and colored her cheeks.

"We talked."

"And?" Charlie's singsong enunciation of the word made Liz laugh.

"And nothing. We talked. Adam went to bed. I stayed up and did a couple of perimeter checks of the house and then I sacked out on the sofa."

The crestfallen expression on Charlie's face made Liz laugh.

"I don't get it," Charlie said. "You guys are perfect for each other. I thought if you had some time to talk privately, you know, catch up on what's been happening over the years, that maybe you guys… Well, you know."

Liz gave Charlie a quick hug. "That's why you're a dog whisperer and not a matchmaker. Stick to what you do best, kiddo."

"Where are you going?"

Liz crossed the lawn and slid behind the wheel of the old pickup truck.

"Where are you going? What do you want me to tell Adam?"

Liz rolled down the window. "Tell him I had to return this truck and then I went to work. I'll see both of you later."

Liz pushed the accelerator of the old pickup as if she were driving a Ferrari instead of a tin can with wheels. She couldn't get away fast enough. Chasing bad guys and fighting crime was a thousand percent easier and more appealing this morning than facing Adam.

Liz entered the observation room where Paul and Sal were conversing. "Fill me in." She gestured to the woman sitting alone behind the large glass window in Interrogation.

"That's Stephanie Murdock, Ms. Willowby's infamous teller who supposedly is having an affair with the bank manager, Joe Grimes." Sal tilted his head. "Paul just told me that Joe Grimes is unable to accept our invitation to join us this morning because he is out of the country on business."

"I checked his travel itinerary, Sheriff. He gets back from Switzerland tomorrow. Darlene and I plan on being his welcome committee."

"Good. Bring him directly to the station, Paul. I want him to have as little heads-up about this as possible." Liz looked through the glass. "Any chance we can keep Miss Hot Pants from tipping him off? I'd like to catch him unaware, if possible."

"We could always arrest her."

"On what charge?"

"Resisting arrest? Failure to yield in a school zone? I'll think of something."

"We're not arresting her, Sal."

"Okay. Okay." He raised his hands in mock surrender. "I'll come up with something else. I have personal family knowledge on ways to encourage people not to talk. I don't have a good Italian name like Sal Rizzo for nothing."

Liz shook her head and laughed out loud. "Stop clowning around and get in there."

"Yes, boss." He gave her a mock salute and left with Paul.

Liz stood, arms folded, behind the two-way glass and watched as Sal worked his magic.

"Let's go over this again, Ms. Murdock. Are you going to try to deny that you and Grimes are having an affair?"

"We're not. I swear."

"It's not a good thing to swear in front of my face, Stephanie. And don't forget that God's watching."

Liz smiled. She knew the God reference had been for her benefit. Sal had been trying to cajole her out of her pensive mood all morning.

Sal leaned across the table. "Talk to me. Do you really want me to think that someone as pretty as you wouldn't have caught the boss's eye?"

Liz's smile widened. Here it comes. Sal's charmschool 101 followed by his she'll-never-know-what-hither trap.

Stephanie preened a little beneath the unexpected compliment. "He might have noticed me."

"See, that's what I'm talking about. Of course he noticed a sweet-looking gal like you." Sal smiled wide, showing off those even white teeth of his. "And I'm sure you were flattered when an important man like Joe Grimes, bank manager, bigwig in high society, took notice of you."

Stephanie stared at Sal for a minute as though weighing her reply.

"Maybe. A little."

"Oh, come on, Stephanie. You're killing me here. Do you really think I'm stupid enough to think that you were nothing more to Joey boy than one of his tellers?"

Stephanie dropped her eyes. "I was one of his tellers. I worked for Mr. Grimes at the Third National Bank. But you know that already."

"You're right, I do know that." Sal got up and moved around to her side of the table. He perched his hip on the edge and leaned in close. "Want to know what else I know?" He pulled a manila folder across the table and slapped it down in front of her.

Stephanie startled at the sudden movement. The look she shot Sal now wasn't flirtatious or innocent— It was wary and maybe even a little bit afraid.

"I know that we traced more than a hundred telephone calls from your cell phone to his over the past six months."

She sputtered but didn't speak.

"I also know that you have a regular rendezvous scheduled every second Saturday at the Marriott in St. Louis. At least he takes you to nice digs and not a cheap motel." When he saw the hesitation on her face, he patted the folder. "We have copies of the hotel receipts to prove it."

"I don't know what you're talking about. If Mr. Grimes was at that hotel like you said, then he must have been there with his wife…or somebody else, maybe… But he wasn't there with me. I can't remember the last time I was in St. Louis."

"Well, maybe I can refresh your memory." The nice-guy tone was gone from his voice and he leaned so close to her face their noses almost touched. "Stop lying to me!"

She jumped and pushed herself farther back in her chair.

"Is this a picture of you?"

The woman's eyes darted to the eight-by-ten picture Sal had pulled from inside his manila folder. Her breathing became labored and she got the trapped look in her eyes that Liz had seen before when a culprit realized they were running out of believable lies.

"We have the names and addresses of a half-dozen people who identified your photo from a wide selection of other photos we offered. They placed you in that hotel with Mr. Grimes the Saturday before last."

Sal's voice almost became a sneer. "Next time you try to be inconspicuous, Stephanie, you might try wearing something other than a flesh-colored see-through dress. The men we showed these pictures to didn't have any trouble at all remembering you. Neither did their wives. Picture jog your memory, sweetheart?"

Her voice hitched and she breathed in short pants. "I want a lawyer."

"Good idea, honey. 'Cause you're going to need one." Sal moved toward the door.

Liz stepped out of the room and met him in the hallway.

"Good job, Sal. At least we've got enough evidence to prove the two of them were having an affair. I'm still having a hard time believing that was motive enough for the Henderson murders."

Sal shrugged. "She's holding something back. I'll let her sit there and stew for a while and then I'll take another crack at her."

"She asked for a lawyer."

"She did?" He pounded the side of his head as he walked away. "Are you sure about that, boss? I thought she said she wanted to call her employer." He grinned and ducked around the corner.

Liz chuckled. She knew she didn't have to worry about Sal. He'd call a public defender for Stephanie, but who could blame him for having a friendly chat with the woman while they waited for the lawyer to arrive?

TWELVE

Deep in thought, Liz drove the last few miles to the Granger estate, or maybe she should start thinking of it as Luke's House. She'd been anxious and uptight about seeing Adam again after the bomb he'd dropped on her about her father and about his feelings for her.

But she should have known better.

Adam didn't bring the subject up again and neither did she.

The past four days Adam had been funny...and warm... and kind...and attentive. Charlie and Adam entertained her each night with tales of life on a Montana ranch with more dogs than horses. Rerun and Jeremy seemed attached at the hip. The boy laughed frequently and even began speaking to them instead of just Rerun.

Adam made his presence, and his intentions, known with subtle movements. The feel of his arm across her shoulders when he'd welcome her each evening in the driveway and escort her into the house. The brush of his fingers on her face when he'd push an errant strand of hair out of her eyes. The smoldering look of his eyes. His never-ending tender smile. The masculine scent of his skin when he'd sit beside her or lean over her. The whole package was intoxicating—and Liz was enjoying every second of it.

She had made up her mind. She was going to steal some private time with him tonight, open her heart and take a leap of faith that he wouldn't break it again. She was going to ask forgiveness for her role in the past, offer forgiveness for his and confess that she wanted a chance to see what the future held for them.

She had never expected a little child to find a crack in her armor—but he had. And once Adam had discovered the crack, he'd been working nonstop to break that crack wide open.

Thank God he had.

She turned down the driveway to the house. She was painting different scenarios in her mind about tonight, when she glanced in her rearview mirror. She slammed her foot on the accelerator and sped toward the house as quickly as possible.

She'd barely pulled to a stop when she leaped from her Smart car, ran around to the passenger side, drew her weapon and waited. She couldn't believe that, as careful as she'd been the past few days, someone had still managed to follow her. She'd switched vehicles. She'd left town, driving in the opposite direction for miles before circling back. She'd checked her rearview mirror more frequently than she'd watched the road ahead.

Yet, when she'd turned into the driveway a few minutes ago her eyes had caught the glint of the sun reflecting off metal behind her. The crunch of gravel and a significant dust cloud announced the car's approach.

She readied her Glock and took aim. Sweat beaded on her forehead. Her pulse raced and she could feel her heart thundering in her chest. She should never have tried to protect Jeremy on her own. Thanks to her stupidity there would be no backup. The only thing standing between that child and a bullet was her.

Whoever was coming up the driveway wasn't trying to conceal their approach. She began to breathe a little easier. Admittedly, there wasn't anywhere to hide a car on this property. No woods to creep through. And if they parked on the main road for a quick getaway, they'd have to walk across several acres of open land to reach the house. Still, the driver was taking his time and didn't appear to be trying to surprise anyone.

When Liz spotted the flasher bar on top of the vehicle, she holstered her weapon, walked back to the driver's side of the car and waited. She folded her arms across her chest and gave her most intimidating glare as the patrol car pulled to a stop less than a half-dozen steps away.

Tom Miller, wearing mirrored sunglasses and dressed in his uniform, stepped from the vehicle and sauntered toward her.

"What are you doing here? Why did you follow me?" Anger laced her words. "How dare you."

"Now, don't get yourself all worked up, Sheriff. I didn't follow you. Not exactly, that is."

"What do you mean you didn't follow me? You're here, aren't you? How did you locate us?"

Tom glanced over her shoulder at the house. "'Us'? Is this where you're stashing Morgan and the kid?"

Liz took a menacing step forward. "Do you like your job, Tom? Because if you don't start explaining yourself in the next ten seconds, you're not going to have one, so make it good." She stood toe to toe with her deputy. "And take off those stupid sunglasses. You're not a Hollywood superstar and you know I hate not being able to see into a person's eyes."

He removed his glasses.

"Now, talk."

"You made a mistake, Sheriff, hiding that kid out here and not telling anyone where he is. How can we help if you keep us in the dark?"

"If I needed your help, Tom, I would have asked for it. How did you find me? I didn't tell you where I was."

Tom walked to the back of her Smart car, reached down, removed a tiny transmitter and held it up for her to see. "Your daddy taught me everything he knew. He was the best sheriff this county ever had—besides you, of course. He would never have forgiven me if I didn't keep an eye on you when I thought you was gettin' in over your head."

Liz did a slow boil but managed to keep a calm outward demeanor. She held out her hand. "Deputy Miller, give me that transmitter."

He handed it over.

"We've got a bad apple on our team, Sheriff. Rotten to the core."

"What are you talking about?" Liz blinked a couple of times trying to process what he was saying.

"I know it ain't easy news to hear. I understand. It wasn't easy for me, either, when I found out. But you need to know, Sheriff. And you're gonna need help taking care of that boy."

Tom cupped his thumbs into his utility belt. "I've found out who the killer is, Sheriff. And I've got the proof to back it up." He stared right into her eyes. "It's Sal Rizzo."

Liz's first reaction was to laugh.

"You won't be laughing none when you see the proof for yourself."

Proof? That Sal was a killer?

When she saw that Tom was deadly serious, her stomach clenched as if she'd been physically punched in the gut. Her eyes widened and her lungs froze, the pain in her chest so intense she thought she might never take a breath again.

"One of my snitches identified him from a photo lineup," Tom said. "He was seen in the alley behind Smitty's the night that drug dealer was killed."

"You're crazy." Liz couldn't help herself. She took a step back as if she were trying to evade a lunatic. "What were you doing showing pictures of cops in a photo lineup, anyway?"

"I weren't out to catch a cop. I was after somebody else and I needed some pictures so I slipped in Sal's and Paul's just so I'd have enough pictures for the guy to look at and give a valid ID."

"I don't believe any of this."

"I know it's hard for you to swallow, Sheriff, you and Sal being close and all. But it's true."

The rush of blood to her head made her temples pound. Her heartbeat sounded in her ears and drowned out his words.

No. This was impossible. Not Sal. Never Sal.

"You're wrong. If you have a witness placing Sal in that alley then there's a good explanation for it. He was probably making an arrest."

"I checked the records. They're clean. No one was brought in that night…or the night before or after. Definitely no drug deals on the books."

"He told me he's working on something," Liz replied. "He probably was questioning a suspect or…or setting up a sting."

"Or buying drugs?"

Liz shook her head from side to side. No. Her mind

and her heart couldn't conceive of Sal betraying her this way.

"Sheriff, the way I've pieced it together, Sal Rizzo developed a drug problem about nine months ago. It's been getting worse and he's been needing more and more of the stuff to feed his habit. He met up with my snitch and the drug dealer in the back of Smitty's bar that night for a buy. The dealer got cocky. He doubled the price on Rizzo. They fought. Rizzo killed him. Didn't mean to. It was an accident. But the guy's dead just the same, ain't he?"

Tom shrugged, folded his arms across his chest and leaned back against his patrol car. "My snitch ran for his life. Went underground. It's taken me weeks and a lot of greased palms to find him."

Liz's gaze darted wildly around the yard. Jeremy's swing sitting idle. The family of ducks in the distance gliding by on the pond. Pots of geraniums hanging from the front porch just as she'd suggested. Everything quiet. Everything normal. But a gut-wrenching fear took root in her soul and she knew from this day forward she'd never be able to believe in normal again.

"Think about it, Sheriff. Rizzo's been handling the investigation of this case. He hasn't had any leads for us. Ain't that right?"

"I don't believe any of this. Who is this snitch? I want him brought in. I want to interview him myself."

"No problem. I'll arrange it. But he's gonna want immunity for his testimony. He's pretty nervous about snitching on a cop."

Tears burned the backs of her eyes and her throat threatened to close.

Please, God. Help me. This can't be happening. Not Sal.

Liz closed her eyes and took several long, deep breaths. She leaned against her Smart car before she collapsed but still fought with everything in her not to let Tom see how devastated she was by his news. When she turned her head and looked at him, she'd have given anything to be able to snatch those stupid mirrored glasses out of his pocket and hide the pain she knew he'd see in her eyes.

"I suppose you're going to try to tell me that Sal is responsible for the Henderson murders, too?" Her strained voice barely squeezed out the question.

Tom shrugged. "Haven't figured that one out yet. But we did find a bag of cocaine under the mattress. There's some kind of drug connection. We just don't know yet what it is. But there's something there. Too coincidental, don't you think? A cop kills a drug dealer…and then that same cop is involved in the investigation of these other two killings that have some connection to drugs. Yet, he hasn't been able to find any usable evidence in either case. Smells fishy to me. Would have raised your daddy's hackles, for sure."

Liz bristled beneath the last remark.

"I want you to leave, Tom. Right this minute. Pick up that snitch and have him waiting for me at the station and don't you utter one word, not one word, do you hear me, to anyone about this. Especially not a word about this location or I'll have your badge."

"Will do, Sheriff."

Before either of them could move, a sharp, piercing scream filled the air. Both of them looked toward the house. Jeremy stood in the doorway, his eyes wide and his hands slapped against his cheeks, and he screamed again.

Liz shot a look at Tom. "Your uniform. I told you never to wear a uniform around Jeremy."

"I'm sorry. I wasn't thinking. I was just trying to get you alone so I could tell you what I found out. I didn't know you were with the boy."

The second Jeremy started screaming, Rerun started barking and howling. Charlie and Adam joined the group at the door and both of them were shouting above the din in an attempt to calm Jeremy and silence Rerun.

Liz threw her hands over her ears and screamed at Tom, "Go! Get out of here now. Don't you open your mouth about any of this. If you do, I promise you'll be on the unemployment line so fast you won't ever see that pension you keep talking about."

"I know you're not happy about the news, Sheriff, but you don't have to be mad at me for delivering it."

"Just go!"

Tom pushed off from the car and hurried to the driver's side.

Before he could slide inside the vehicle, Liz yelled, "You better have that snitch waiting for me in the interrogation room when I get there. Understand?"

Tom nodded and within seconds all she saw were taillights and dust clouds disappearing in the distance.

Fighting the roiling of her stomach and the taste of bile in her mouth, Liz turned toward the chaos in the house. She sprinted up the porch steps and flung open the door. Charlie had silenced Rerun and had him lying quietly at Jeremy's feet. This time neither Adam nor Rerun had been able to subdue Jeremy and, to her surprise, the crying child threw himself at her.

She dropped to her knees and embraced the boy. She held him tightly, remembering what Adam had told her about the calming effects of swaddling. "It's okay, Jeremy. Shh. It's okay."

Rerun whined and squirmed a bit. The dog wanted to try to soothe Jeremy as he'd been trained to do but Charlie enforced her "stay" command.

Adam closed the front door and took control of the situation. "I think everyone needs to move into the living room, sit down and regroup. It's been a highly upsetting few minutes and we need to catch our breath and discuss what happened out there."

Agreeing with his assessment of the situation, Liz stood up, still clutching Jeremy tightly in her arms. She crossed into the living room and settled into the nearest rocking chair and rocked.

Charlie perched on the arm of the nearest sofa and waited for Liz to explain.

"What's going on?" Adam shot her a perplexed look. "How did Tom Miller know our location? I thought we agreed that no one would know about this location but the three of us."

Liz heard the exasperation and tinge of anger in his voice.

"I didn't tell him."

"He followed you?" Charlie's eyes looked like saucers. "But aren't you his boss? Isn't it a big no-no to sneak around and follow your boss?" Before Liz could answer, she leaned forward. "You're going to fire him, right? I never liked that guy, anyway. He's old as the hills and walks around like a cowboy from a Clint Eastwood spaghetti western. It's time to put him out to pasture, don't you think?"

Leave it to Charlie to bring a smile to her face—if only for the briefest moment. Her eyes shot to Adam.

"I didn't tell him our location. He put a tracking device on the bumper of my car."

"Wow! That's definitely grounds to kick his butt to the curb."

"Charlie!" Both of them shouted her name in unison.

She threw her hands up in the air. "Okay, I get it. I'll leave the two of you to talk and I'll take the dog out to do his business. I don't know if the chaos excited his bladder or not but it did a number on mine." She stood up, signaled Rerun and started walking toward the back door. They could hear her muttering under her breath as she left, "Just when things start to get exciting they always send you and me away, Rerun."

Adam shook his head.

"There's only one Charlie."

"Thank God."

Both of them laughed.

Liz looked down at the child nestled in her arms. The slow rhythm of the rocker had lulled him to sleep. He looked younger than his five years. She traced a finger down his soft skin and inhaled the lingering scent of baby shampoo on his hair. She'd fallen in love with this child, so much that just the thought of anything happening to him brought her to her knees.

"Here." Adam lifted the boy from her arms. "Let me lay him down. He's had a rough morning. I'll be right back."

When he was gone, Liz replayed the morning's events in her mind. Could it be true? Had Sal accidentally killed the drug dealer? She still couldn't wrap her mind around even the possibility of such an event.

But Tom had a witness.

Insofar as a drug-addicted snitch could be considered a reliable witness.

But if the man had been there and witnessed the fight…

The more she thought about it, as much as she didn't want to admit it, the more the story seemed possible. Sal was the lead investigator on the drug dealer homicide. He'd been very mysterious about this hunch of his and he had offered her very little information when pressed about it. He hadn't turned up any viable leads in either the drug dealer or the Henderson homicides. Yet, he was front and center in each investigation, able to manipulate evidence, possibly cover his tracks, so he'd know exactly what they had—and what they didn't.

Still, this was Sal they were talking about. Her best friend. Her right hand.

"Penny for your thoughts." Adam stood in the doorway, his shoulder leaning against the door frame, his arms crossed, his gaze probing.

"Not this time, Adam. Not now." She sprang to her feet. "I've got to go."

"Liz, wait. Something's going on. Something really difficult for you." He stood in front of her. "I've been told I'm a good listener if you want to talk about it."

She shook her head no.

He reached out and tugged at her hand. When she was standing close enough to see his eyes, he said, "I have faith in you, Lizzie Bradford. You're one of the smartest, bravest women I've ever met. Whatever you're wrestling with, you're strong enough to get through it. When you do, just remember I'll be right here, waiting for you when it's over."

She didn't want him to be kind right now or understanding for fear she'd break down crying and not be able to stop. She offered him a feeble smile, brushed past him and hurried out to her car.

"Liz?"

He had followed her onto the porch.

When she turned, she knew he'd see the tears streaming down her cheeks but it didn't matter. Nothing mattered but getting back to the station and finding out if it was true. "I have to go."

THIRTEEN

Sal was sprawled in a chair in her office waiting for her when she arrived at the station. She tried not to meet his eyes and circled behind her desk. "What are you doing here?"

"Waiting for you."

"How'd you know I was coming in to the office?"

Sal alerted. Nothing got past him. He sat up straight and stared at her. "What's the matter with you? Get out of bed and walk into a wall?"

Where were Tom's mirrored sunglasses when she needed them? She couldn't look at Sal. She couldn't let him see the doubt and the suspicion in her eyes.

"I'm not in the mood for jokes. Have Darlene and Paul left yet for the airport to pick up Grimes?"

She could feel his probing gaze.

"No. I saw Paul in the break room just a couple of minutes ago. Darlene was at her desk looking at files." His words were clipped and she heard the undercurrent of anger lacing them. "Something wrong, boss?"

She straightened her shoulders and glared at him.

"How did you know I was coming in to the station?"

"I was walking past Dispatch when you called it in." He stood up and returned her stare. "What's going on?"

"I want you to drive out to the airport and pick up Grimes."

"But Paul—"

"You do it, Sal. I have another assignment for Paul. Take Darlene with you."

"I don't understand. You—"

"What's there to understand? I just gave you a direct order. Now do it."

An angry red flush crept up his neck. He looked like he wanted to say something but fought to refrain from doing it. He stared hard at her. "Anything you say, boss." He spit the words through clenched teeth and sauntered out of the room.

Liz collapsed into her chair.

It was not true. Couldn't be true.

Taking a deep breath, she stood up again and headed to the interrogation room to speak with Tom's snitch. It was time to find out.

Who did she think she was talking to him like that? He didn't give a rat's butt if she was his boss or not. Nobody talked to him like that and got away with it. Nobody.

His fingers tapped his gun.

Enough was enough.

He'd decided long ago he was going to kill the boy. If the sheriff had been killed in the car crash, it would have been collateral damage. But not anymore.

She was a target now. One he could hardly wait to bring down.

Liz didn't know how long she'd been staring out the window—no more than a few minutes, but it felt like hours, seeing everything, registering nothing. She felt dead inside, as if her heart had stopped beating and she was only a shell of a human being.

She needed to turn in her badge.

She couldn't trust herself to make good decisions anymore. She had been wrong about both Adam and his father. She had misread signs that might have saved Luke. She had tried so hard to be the "son" her father wanted, even devoted her life to following in his footsteps, made excuses for some of his decisions, overlooked his moments of cruelty. She had been wrong to put him on a pedestal.

She had loved her father…she loved him still…but he had been human with character flaws she had refused to acknowledge.

She had proven herself to be a terrible judge of character.

And now…

How could she have been so wrong about Sal?

She could hear his voice coming down the hall, heard him joking with the dispatcher, teasing Paul as he passed. She swiveled her chair around to greet him.

Sal poked his head into her office and hung on the doorjamb. "Boss, I put Grimes in interrogation room one. You want to do the interview or do you want me to do it?"

"You do it. I'll observe."

Sal hesitated, straightened up and stepped into the office. He glanced over his shoulder and started to close the door.

"Don't. Leave it open."

He shot her a questioning glance. "I just wanted to speak to you privately for a moment."

Liz pushed her chair away from her desk and stood

up. "It will have to wait. Don't you have an interview waiting for you?"

He stepped closer.

"You've been crying." It wasn't a question. "Liz… Let me help."

"Detective Rizzo, you have an interview to conduct. I suggest you do it."

He jerked his head back as if she had physically slapped him. She could hardly bear the hurt she saw in his eyes. Giving her a mock salute, he headed out the door without another word.

Liz followed behind, her feet dragging like they were encased in cement. She took her place behind the two-way mirror in the observation room.

Sal sat with his back to the mirror. His body language and the force he used to slap the folder on the table in front of him revealed his seething anger.

She understood. She was angry and hurt, too. Everything that Tom told her, the snitch had verified. The man had been scared out of his mind during the interrogation. It didn't take a load of brain cells to figure out that snitching on a cop to the sheriff was the last thing he wanted to do. But once the D.A. had agreed to immunity, snitch he did. He gave dates, places, times that Sal supposedly met with the dealer to buy drugs prior to the murder. He gave specifics of the crime that only someone present when the murder occurred could know.

Liz had personally pulled all the Dispatch records and time sheets looking for something, anything, that would prove Sal couldn't have done these horrible things. If she could place him on a call or in the office or anything…

None of the times the snitch gave her—not one—

could she place Sal in a legitimate spot doing police business.

She had to face facts. There were no leads in an investigation Sal was heading. He had no alibi for the time of the murder or for the alleged buy times. There was an eyewitness ready to testify against him.

But was it enough to prove that her most valuable detective—and best friend—was a murderer? Was it enough to arrest him and humiliate him in front of his peers? Put his career in jeopardy and his reputation in question? If he was innocent and she arrested him, even when cleared, suspicion would linger over his head for years. Most people believed the old adage "where there's smoke, there's fire."

And if she didn't?

Convictions had been won with less circumstantial evidence than she had already collected. Could she really turn a blind eye to what was staring her in the face simply because this time the case hit closer to home?

The one thing she was absolutely sure about was that she couldn't risk Jeremy's safety—not even to protect Sal.

For now, she was going to watch this interview. She stared at Joe Grimes through the glass. He was a man in his mid-forties, with a slight touch of gray at his temples, a little thickening through his waist, a man losing hold of youth and primed for a midlife crisis. Could she believe he'd decided to have a fling with a twenty-something teller in his employ? Yes. But was he a cold-blooded killer?

Never before had she hoped so hard that that would prove to be true.

"How was your trip to Zurich, Mr. Grimes?" Sal spoke to the man in a friendly, relaxed manner, as though Grimes were a long-lost friend he was welcoming back from vacation. "Was the trip business or pleasure?"

"Business."

"Really? That's funny. I checked with the bank. They told me that you took a couple of personal days. Then I checked with your wife and she told me that you were away on business. So, which was it? Business or pleasure?"

Joe shifted in his chair. Liz could almost see the wheels turning in his head as he weighed his words.

"What's this all about? Why am I here?"

So, he'd decided to go on the defensive. Good. Sal was a master at this type of chess game.

"Just answer the question, sir."

Grimes pushed back from the table, propped an ankle on the opposite knee and clasped his hands on the knee. He was trying to appear nonchalant, unconcerned. It wasn't working.

"It was business...personal business."

Sal nodded his head, flipped open the manila folder in front of him and took an excessive amount of time to read the contents.

"You can't just keep me here." Grimes blustered, dropping both feet to the floor and waving an index finger at Sal. "I know my rights. Tell me right now why you are detaining me."

Sal closed the folder and went for the jugular. "You've been having an affair with Stephanie Murdock for over six months. When were you planning on telling your wife?"

The bluster went out of Joe Grimes as quickly as if someone had popped a balloon, but still he tried to hold on to the lie.

"I don't know what you're talking about."

"You don't know about the every-other-Saturday rendezvous at the Marriott in St. Louis? You don't know about the diamond bracelet and watch placed on your personal charge card?"

Sal stood and picked up the folder.

"Okay, I'll go next door and have this same conversation with your wife. Maybe I'm mistaken. Maybe the diamonds were a gift for her."

Sal had his hand on the doorknob before Grimes recovered enough to speak.

"Wait!"

Sal paused at the door but didn't come back inside.

"Yes. I've been having an affair." The man dropped his head and his shoulders slumped forward.

Sal crossed the room and sat back down at the table. "Now let's keep telling the truth, okay?"

Grimes nodded.

"How long have you been seeing Ms. Murdock."

"Seven months."

"Were you intending to leave your wife?"

"No, of course not." Fear shone from his eyes. "Whoever told you that lied. I love my wife. I would never leave her."

"Just cheat on her, is that it?"

"Look, I'm sorry. I'm ashamed of what I've done. It…it just happened."

"Tell me about the argument you had with Mr. Henderson."

Grimes looked shocked. He sat up straight in his chair and just blinked.

"You did have an argument with David Henderson on August twenty-second, didn't you, Mr. Grimes?"

"We…I…" His eyes darted around the room before

he settled down, took a deep breath and came clean. "Yes, David and I had words."

"About Ms. Murdock?

"Yes. I'd given Henderson keys to my office so he could install a new financial software package on my computer after hours. He mixed up the date that I expected him to come and discovered Stephanie and I…"

"Why did your dalliances bother Henderson?"

"They didn't, really. Let's face it, he's a man. He knew how it was. He was more concerned about his own butt."

Sal arched an eyebrow.

"If his wife found out he knew about us and didn't tell… That's really why he was pushing the issue."

"Where were you the night of August fifteenth?"

Grimes looked up and shot him a puzzled look.

"What?"

"August fifteenth. Saturday night, three weeks ago. Does Smitty's bar ring a bell?"

"Smitty's bar?" Grimes twisted his face like he'd just been presented with a foul odor. "I wouldn't be caught dead in that place."

"Funny you should say that. Somebody was found dead behind the bar on August fifteenth."

Liz flattened her hand against the glass. This was it. The moment of truth. Every other suspect had been cleared. Grimes had to be the killer. Otherwise…

Please. Let it be you. Please. Please.

"I was at a charity function in St. Louis on August fifteenth with my wife. More than a hundred people will back that up. I was one of the guest speakers."

She hadn't been aware she was holding her breath until Grimes produced an ironclad alibi and the air burst from her lungs.

Liz pushed back from the glass and fought for composure. Grimes had been her last hope. Now she'd be forced to make a decision that once made could never be taken back.

She stared at Sal through the mirror and a thousand other scenarios rushed through her head. Sal slouching in front of her desk, handing her her morning coffee with just the right amount of cream and sugar, gun drawn and at her back more than once, sitting at her side through thick and thin. A sounding board. A clown. A partner. A dear, dear friend.

Adam's words from last night rang in her head. *"I have faith in you, Lizzie. You're one of the smartest, bravest women I've ever met. Whatever you're wrestling with, you're strong enough to get through it. When you do, I'll be right here, waiting for you when it's over."*

Liz glanced through the glass once more. The thought of having to cuff Sal and put him behind bars soured her stomach and broke her heart. But she had to do what she had to do.

While Sal continued the interview, Liz took the opportunity to slip into the restroom. She used the facilities, threw some water on her face and braced herself for what was ahead. Releasing the cuffs from her belt, she headed to the interrogation room.

She threw open the door. The room was empty.

Liz hurried toward the front of the office just in time to see Mr. Grimes, head bowed, walking out the front door.

"Darlene, what's going on? Where's Sal?"

"He told me to release Mr. Grimes and he ran out of here. Said he had someplace important he had to be."

Someplace important?

Liz raced for the door, pulling her cell phone from her pocket as she ran.

Please, Lord. Keep them safe. Let me get there in time.

FOURTEEN

Adam stood on the front porch. He didn't have long to wait. Liz's patrol car, kicking up clouds of dust, fishtailed in the turn of the driveway and skidded to a stop.

He jumped off the three porch steps, rushed around to the driver's side and had the door open before she had released her seat belt.

"What's wrong? All you said on the phone was 'pack and be ready to go.'"

Liz brushed past him toward the house with Adam in tow.

"Did you do it? Are you packed?"

Adam caught up with her, grabbed her arm and spun her around.

"Lizzie, talk to me. What's going on?"

"I'll explain in the car. We've got to get out of here right now. Please tell me you've packed."

Her eyes revealed her panic and fear. She started to turn away but he held her firmly in place.

"Liz, stop."

She looked at him. The expression on her face shook him to the core. This wasn't tough, stoic, in-control Sheriff Bradford. Something bad had happened. But what?

"Sweetheart, take a deep breath. Calm down and talk to me."

Perhaps it was the endearment that caught her off guard, or maybe it was the deep concern that she could probably see in his eyes, or maybe the gentleness of his voice, but the dam finally broke and this hard-as-nails tough cop broke down into a sobbing, scared, vulnerable woman. "I've been so wrong, Adam…about everything…about everyone."

"Shh. It will be okay." He folded her into his arms. The trembling of her body made him deepen his embrace. All he wanted to do was protect her, shelter her. "Whatever it is, we'll work it out…together. But you need to calm down and talk to me."

She clutched the front of his shirt and looked up at him. Her eyes shimmered like two beautiful blue lakes overflowing their banks.

"Is Jeremy okay?"

"Of course. Charlie and Rerun are with him. They're upstairs packing."

She swiveled her head and looked toward the horizon, her eyes scanning the yard and the neighboring fields of tall grass.

"Has anyone been here? Have you received any phone calls in the past hour or so? Even sales calls. Tell me if you did."

"No, Liz. No one came. No one called. Just you." He released his hold. His brow furrowed and a frown pulled at his mouth. "I can't help you if you don't tell me what's wrong."

She tugged at his hand. "Inside. It isn't safe out here."

They moved into the living room. Liz raced to the window, stood to the side and edged the lace curtain aside. When he saw her hand rest on her gun, he didn't wait for an explanation. Immediately, he withdrew a key from his pocket, crossed to the fireplace, unlocked the box on the mantel and withdrew his Glock.

Liz glanced over her shoulder. "What are you doing? Put that away. I don't have eyes in the back of my head, Adam. I can't watch everything and everyone. I have enough to worry about without you walking around with a loaded gun."

"Good. Then you can concentrate on whatever threat you think is going to come up that driveway. You know I have the necessary permits to carry this and, even though you haven't seen me in action, I assure you that I could give you a run for your money on any target range."

He crossed the room and stood slightly behind her on the left, close enough to be able to shoot out the window if necessary, far enough behind that he wouldn't distract her or make her feel she'd have to split her attention to protect him.

The air had a palpable tension, yet he refused to question her further. She reminded him of a stallion he'd once seen Bob work with back on the Montana ranch. He had been trying to domesticate the animal, get it used to the feel of a saddle on its back, then slowly the weight of a man. He never forgot the panicked, wild look in the animal's eyes as it rose on its hind legs, striking the air with its forelegs, fighting an invisible threat for its survival.

He saw that panicked, wild look in Liz's eyes now.

So, he did what Bob had done. He stayed close but gave her space. He gave her enough rope to think she was free yet kept hold tight enough to control the situation if necessary. And he waited.

And just like the stallion that fought and reared and

paced, when adrenaline no longer raced through Liz's bloodstream, she regained control. Her breathing became deep, slow, steady breaths instead of hyperventilating pants. Her spine straightened. She threw her shoulders back.

Adam knew from her body language the instant Liz had found her tough-as-nails sheriff persona and had put it back on. His assessment was confirmed when she turned and locked her gaze with his.

"I've called in the federal marshals. We can't protect Jeremy any longer. I've asked them to put him in the witness protection program."

Adam blinked hard. He hadn't known what to expect but it hadn't been this, and it took a minute to deal with the surprise.

"They're going to meet us in town, at the back door of Mrs. Willowby's general store in two hours."

"Mrs. Willowby's? Not the sheriff's office?"

"No one will expect us to be meeting at her place. Even Mrs. Willowby doesn't have a clue we're coming her way. There's an alley between buildings and a second alley between the back of her home and two standalone garages in the back. It's an easily protected and safe place to make the switch."

All her senses were on alert but, after one more scan of the grounds, she seemed satisfied that she had made it to the house before the person she expected and that they weren't in imminent danger—yet.

"Are you packed?"

"I can be. I didn't know whether an overnight bag was sufficient. Apparently, you had a more lengthy departure in mind. I'll put Charlie in the loop and be right back."

He took the stairs two at a time, told Charlie what

he needed from her and returned downstairs to find a much more relaxed, in-control Liz in the kitchen. She'd actually put on a pot of coffee.

"I'm sorry I panicked before." She offered a tremulous smile. "I thought I was too late. I thought he'd beaten me out here." She raised a cup. "Coffee?"

"Liz, you're driving me crazy. You show up in a panic, refuse to answer any of my questions, insist we leave immediately, and now you're asking me if I want a cup of coffee?" Adam laughed. "I deal with crazies for a living, and you, sweetheart, are moving to the head of the list fast."

Liz chuckled and poured him a cup.

"I know. I told you that I panicked and overreacted. But I'm pretty sure that we're safe for the moment. Besides, I sent for reinforcements. Darlene and Paul should be here any moment."

"So much for keeping this place a secret. I should have known. What's that old saying? How do you spread a message the fastest? Telephone, telegraph and tell a woman."

Liz swatted his arm. "That's not fair. Until Tom put a bug on my car, I was very careful and discreet about this place."

He nodded and took a mouthful of coffee. The rich aroma and deep-flavored taste helped settle the nerves she'd thrown into high gear when she'd shown up with her "Chicken Little, the sky is falling" scenario.

"Now that you've calmed down and have returned to a modicum of sanity, would you like to tell me what's going on? Why WITSEC? What happened?"

Her eyes glistened and he was afraid she was going to lose it again, but she didn't. She compartmentalized her emotions and all he saw looking back at him now was Sheriff Bradford.

"We have identified a prime suspect in the murder of a local drug dealer. We have circumstantial evidence and a strong reason to believe that particular homicide is also tied in with the Henderson murders."

Adam raised his coffee cup but stopped halfway to his mouth at that bombshell of a statement.

"The final ballistics report on the weapon used to shoot out the tires of my car came in, too."

Her gaze locked with his.

"The bullets were fired from a departmental-issued sniper rifle."

Adam lowered his cup to the counter before he dropped it.

"Police rifle?"

"It's Sal, Adam." A fleeting glimpse of pain shot through her eyes but she didn't waver. "Sal is our killer."

"Sal?" Adam laughed. "That's ridiculous. Where did you get a crazy idea like that? Sal might be a lot of things—narcissistic, competitive, jealous—but a cold-blooded killer? No way. He's too doggone proud of being a detective. Wherever you got your information, Liz, you're wrong."

"I understand how you feel. I had major reservations myself. But the evidence is piling up and everything points to Sal—including an eyewitness to the drug dealer's murder."

"I don't care if you have ten eyewitnesses. I've come to know Sal. He's a good guy who puts on a tough-guy Italian stereotype bravado. He would never hurt a kid." Adam looked long and hard at her. "And he'd never do anything to hurt you."

Liz dropped her eyes and sighed heavily. "I feel the

same way, Adam. I can't believe Sal did this. I can't. But when I finally decided to arrest him and let the courts get to the bottom of it all, he took off."

"What do you mean he took off?"

"He knew something was up, that I was terribly upset about something. He kept pushing me to try to find out what it was. When I didn't budge, he must have put two and two together. I stepped into the ladies' room to compose myself. When I came out, he was gone. Told Darlene he had someplace important he had to be."

"That doesn't mean—"

"He didn't give his location to the dispatcher. He didn't take a patrol car so we couldn't track his GPS."

Adam's brow furrowed. "There has to be another explanation, Liz. I'm a decent judge of character—make my living at it—and Sal's is stellar."

"No! Get back here. Rerun, no!"

At the sound of Charlie's chastisement, followed by the thump, thump, thump of dog and people racing down the stairs, Adam and Liz rushed into the foyer. They got there just in time to see Charlie and Rerun in a tug-of-war for Jeremy's teddy bear while Jeremy, a wide grin on his face, sat on the steps watching as if this was happening for his entertainment.

Charlie won. She shook her finger at Rerun. "I don't get it. This is the one area I just can't get this dog to obey. He won't leave this bear alone. He keeps ripping it out of Jeremy's hands."

She smoothed her hand over the stuffed toy, wiping the wet, tousled fur on her clothes and gave the bear back to Jeremy. Charlie plopped down on the steps beside Jeremy. "So, where are we going this time?"

The moment of truth was at hand. Adam knew this wasn't going to be easy for any of them. Goodbyes never were. What Liz didn't realize yet, and he wasn't looking forward to telling her, was that he had to leave, too.

He had no choice. He couldn't just hand the boy over to federal marshals and hope for the best. It would traumatize Jeremy and undo the recovery process he'd set in motion.

Jeremy's new family would need to be trained on how to deal not only with autism but any residual effects Jeremy might suffer from because of the trauma of the last few weeks.

Although Jeremy had just started talking about the "bad man," he hadn't been able to open up and talk about that night.

Yet.

But he would. Adam was sure of it.

He'd promised Liz that very first day that he would protect the child. When he'd moved the boy back into his home, he'd promised that he would be with Jeremy through the recovery process…and he was going to keep that promise.

Sometimes one-hour sessions twice a week weren't enough.

Luke had taught both of them that painful lesson.

But leaving Liz—again. Would the tenuous relationship they had just started to rebuild survive? Would he?

Please, Lord, help her understand.

"I've arranged for Jeremy to be put into WITSEC." Liz glanced at her watch. "We're meeting the marshals in about ninety minutes."

Charlie stood and stared at them. For the first time her mouth hung open and she appeared speechless. She stared at Jeremy, her eyes misting. Then her gaze darted between Adam and Liz.

"WITSEC? That means…"

Liz uncharacteristically wrapped her arms around Charlie and gave her a huge bear hug. "That means, my dear, dear friend, that you get to go home today." When she released her, Liz's eyes shimmered but, still holding on to her sheriff persona, she did not shed a tear. Her voice was stern, controlling. "You will call me...often."

Charlie smiled her signature smile despite the tear that rolled down her cheek. "Try and stop me."

"I've been told you train police dogs. I might be in the market for one."

"Really? I have the perfect pup in mind."

"Good. Next vacation, I'll plan to come and see what a dog-training Montana ranch looks like."

"You better."

Liz glanced at her watch again. "Are you packed?"

"Yes. Keep an eye on Jeremy and I'll run upstairs and get the bags."

Adam tugged Liz's hand. When he had her attention, he broke his news.

"You know that I have to go into WITSEC with Jeremy." She blinked a couple of times. Her face scrunched up and she tilted her head to the side as if she wasn't sure what she'd heard.

"Lizzie, he needs me. This is a crucial point in his recovery. He's lost his parents, been in a horrendous car crash, had to adjust to a house full of strangers, been the victim of a failed abduction. All of this would be traumatic for any child but for one with communication difficulties..."

His let his words fade away while she processed the impact of them.

He tenderly ran his hand down her arm. "I know the timing of all of this stinks. But I can't let him go through this alone. Truthfully, Lizzie, you wouldn't want me to, would you?"

She had a shell-shocked look in her eyes. She glanced at Jeremy and when she looked back at Adam, her maternal instincts were front and center.

"Of course you must go. I don't know why I didn't think of it myself. I don't want Jeremy to have to make this transition alone."

Adam nodded. "I knew you'd understand."

"How long do you think you'll be gone?" Liz made a sweeping motion with her arm. "What about all of this? Your plans for the safe house?"

"It's waited fifteen years. I'm praying it can wait a little longer."

They stared into each other's eyes and knew they weren't just talking about the house.

Liz nodded. "It's a strong house, built on a firm foundation. It will be here when you get back."

Realizing that she would be saying goodbye to the three people in her life that had managed to penetrate that I-don't-need-anyone protective armor she'd surrounded herself with for years, her emotions sprang to the surface and he could see she was having a difficult time keeping them at bay.

"Excuse me. I have to go and make a last-minute check to make sure we're not leaving anything behind," she whispered, barely able to make eye contact with him.

Just our shattered hearts.

He sighed and watched her race up the stairs. A little voice inside his head got louder and stronger. *Turn it over to God. Trust in the power and goodness of the Lord.* And he did.

FIFTEEN

Liz closed the bathroom door and collapsed back against the wood. Could this day get any worse? She'd have to arrest Sal, once she found him. She had to say goodbye to the one true female friend she'd made since high school. She'd never see her precious, precious Jeremy again.

That thought alone plunged a knife right through her heart.

Now Adam was leaving—again.

She understood why. On a deeper level, she even admired him and respected him for his choice.

But to lose him again?

How many times can a heart break?

She knew the answer to that from firsthand experience—a heart can shatter a million times. People leave. Luke did. Her mother did. Adam did.

People disappoint you. People hurt you. But God never will.

Liz whispered a prayer of thanksgiving that Adam had helped her find her way back to the Lord…to depend on the Lord to see her through the storms. She whispered gratitude for the blessings He brought to each day. Even days like this God would use for the greater good. She knew that He would be by her side and give her the strength to let go of Jeremy…of Adam…of Charlie…of Sal, no matter how difficult it would be.

A warm inner peace filled her being. God had heard her prayers.

She dashed water on her face, plastered a Charlie-size smile on her lips, and went downstairs to finish the job she'd started.

She had reached the bottom step when she looked through a pane of glass in the front door and saw a vehicle engulfed in a dust cloud coming up the driveway at a high rate of speed. She motioned everyone into the living room, drew her Glock and took position behind the front door. Once the car screeched to a stop and she could identify the driver, she holstered her weapon and stepped outside.

"Tom. What are you doing here? I'm expecting Darlene and Paul any minute now but I didn't call you."

"They're not coming." He took long, determined strides toward her.

"I don't understand."

"Have you seen Sal?" He climbed the steps and stood beside her.

"No. He left before…" She scrunched her face and chewed on her lower lip. "I haven't seen Sal. Why are you here?"

"You need more than a Barbie doll and a wuss to help you."

Her face colored and she fought to control her temper against this Neanderthal.

"Paul is not—"

Tom placed a hand on her arm.

"Look, Sheriff, I don't have time for you to start with

your politically correct jargon. Now, get the boy and let's get out of here."

Adam stepped onto the porch, the Glock visible in his hand.

"Lizzie? Is there a problem out here?"

Tom instantly released his hold, stepped back and pushed his hat back on his head. "Hi, Doc. Didn't see you standing there."

"Tom." Adam acknowledged the greeting but didn't lower his weapon.

"What's got into you?" Liz brushed her arm where Tom had grabbed it. "What are you doing here? Where are Darlene and Paul?"

"I told them to stay at the station."

"What? Who gave you the right to—"

"Sal did."

Liz stared at him as if he were crazy.

"We're no match for Sal. None of us are and you know it. When I found out he was missing—"

"He's not missing."

"No? Then you know where he is? You have him locked up tight somewhere?"

When Liz didn't immediately answer, Tom said, "That's what I thought. Look, you can dock my pay, ream my butt, doggone it, you can even fire me when all this is over. I don't care. But I need you to grab that kid, get in the car and get out of here before Sal shows up and you and the kid are the ones who are missing."

"He's right, Liz. We need to move." Adam holstered his weapon at his side.

Liz stepped into Tom's personal space and shot him her most intense glare. "You've stepped over the line, Officer Miller...again. Do it again and you're fired."

"Yes, Sheriff. I hear you. Now, can we please get out of here?"

"You get back in the car and scoot down. I don't want Jeremy to spot your uniform. We can't afford a meltdown right now. You can ride shotgun for us."

Liz yelled into the house. "Charlie, I need you to get Jeremy and Rerun settled in the car. We're leaving right now." Her eyes caught Adam's. "You and I will grab the bags and pack the SUV."

Everyone scattered to do her bidding.

Minutes later the bags were loaded into the back of the SUV. Adam closed up the back and walked around to the driver's side.

"I'll lead," Liz shouted, and ran back to her patrol car.

Tom blasted his horn to get her attention. Annoyed, she jogged over to see what he wanted now. He lowered the glass as she approached. She leaned her hands on the door and bent down to see him, face-to-face.

"What now?"

"You drive with them, Sheriff. Leave your car here. The team and I will make sure it gets back to the station."

She opened her mouth to protest when he patted her hand in a fatherly way. "I know how much that boy has come to mean to you. Ride in with him. Take the time to say goodbye."

Her heart clenched. She had such a tiny window of time and then Jeremy would be gone from her life forever. She smiled. "Thanks, Tom."

Liz waved her hand for them to wait and she sprinted toward the vehicle. When she got there, chaos surrounded her. Charlie was wrestling with Rerun. The dog had Jeremy's bear in his mouth and this time was not going to give it up. Jeremy had unlatched his safety belt, climbed out of his car seat and was tugging on the dog. Adam muttered a word she hadn't ever heard him use before, pushed off from the steering wheel and got out of the car.

Liz opened the back door to help get Jeremy back in his car seat. Rerun didn't hesitate. He saw a chance to escape and knocked her backward as he leaped out of the car. Charlie yelled at Rerun, got out the other passenger door and chased the dog through the field. Jeremy scooted across the seat and made his getaway, chasing Charlie and Rerun. Adam helped Liz to her feet and both of them joined the chase.

The whole ridiculous scenario couldn't have taken more than sixty seconds.

But it was sixty seconds that saved their lives.

When the SUV exploded, the ground shook and a massive fireball shot into the sky. The force of the explosion lifted both Adam and Liz off their feet and slammed them to the ground. The impact stole her breath and froze her in place while pain radiated through each strand of hair and coursed down to her toes.

Liz raised her head in time to see Charlie, Rerun and Jeremy huddling together in the tall grass about fifty feet ahead. She turned her head to the left and saw Adam. He had propped himself up on his elbow and was shouting something at her. Her ears rang. His muffled voice sounded like she was underwater.

The heat was intense and seared her skin. Sparks, ash and pieces of metal fell from the sky like fireworks debris.

Adam jumped to his feet and helped her up. Then with his arm wrapped around her waist, they ran as far away from the flames as they could and joined the others. They sat in a huddled group on the ground and watched in shock and amazement.

Tom Miller jumped from his car and ran through the tall grass, too. When he reached them, Liz offered a silent prayer that they were all alive and unhurt.

Then she saw the gun in Tom's hand—pointed right at her heart.

"I can't believe it. You just won't die, will you?"

Adam started to rise but stopped when he saw Tom release the safety on his weapon.

"That's right, Doc. You just set yourself back down nice and easy, now."

Rerun barked furiously and strained wildly at his leash. Charlie had her feet braced on the ground and was trying with all her strength to get the animal under control.

Jeremy didn't cry. He simply stared at Tom. Then he pointed his finger. "Bad man shot Mommy. Bad man. Bad man."

Liz's sharp intake of breath made her shudder and tears sprang to her eyes. She looked from the boy to the man hovering over her…and to his gun pointed inches from her chest.

"Tom? It was you?"

"Do you think I wanted this to happen? Any of it? But things just got out of control. One mistake led to another…and another…and…"

"'Mistake'? You murdered two innocent people in cold blood, Tom."

"It wasn't supposed to happen!" he screamed. "Don't you understand? It all started when I got in a fight with that drug dealer behind Smitty's bar. We were fighting. I pushed him against the wall and he went for my gun. What was I supposed to do, let him kill me?" Tom couldn't hide the hysteria building in his voice. "I covered it up. I thought I was in the clear. But someone else was in the alley that night. They decided to blackmail me. They sent me a picture on my computer at work that they got off the security camera of what I'd done."

Tom stepped closer.

"It's your fault, anyway. You had to have the newest technology—like Country Corners ever needed any of that junk. So, you hired Henderson to install all that computer garbage with screens and GPS in our cars. But that wasn't enough. You wanted new software uploaded to our office computers, too. Henderson was working on my computer. I knew from the expression on his face and how fast he hightailed it out of the office that he'd stumbled upon the picture."

He shrugged a shoulder.

"I didn't go to the house to kill him. I just wanted to talk to him, find out what he knew or thought he knew. But he freaked out. I made a mistake. I wish I hadn't killed him. The whole thing just keeps growing and growing and I just want it all to go away."

"Murder's not a mistake! Dear Lord, Tom, you killed a young boy's parents!" Liz screamed at him and raised herself to a sitting position. Adam inched closer to her.

"Don't move!" Sal stood up from his hiding place in the brush, his gun pointed directly at Tom. He was covered with dirt and sweat and his chest heaved as though he had just run a marathon.

Tom swung his weapon toward Sal, both now in a standoff.

"I wondered when you were going to show up. The great Detective Rizzo, Mr. Hero-To-The-Rescue. Sorry. Today's not hero day." He placed the gun against Liz's head. "Lower your weapon or I'll shoot."

"Don't lower your weapon, Sal. That's an order," Liz yelled.

Tom pressed the barrel harder against her forehead.

"I'm not counting to three, boy. I said do it now."

Slowly Sal lowered his gun to the ground and took a step back.

Rerun rent the air with continuous, frantic, furious barks and strained against his leash despite the choker collar.

"Shut that mutt up!" Tom yelled.

Charlie's voice shook as she commanded Rerun to sit multiple times. But the dog was out of control. He ripped the leash out of her hand and lunged toward Tom, who took a startled step back…

A gunshot sounded.

The dog yelped.

Silence.

Then everything happened at once. Both Jeremy and Charlie screamed and threw themselves on top of the fallen dog. Adam sprang up and lunged himself at Tom. Tom turned and pointed his gun at Adam's chest.

Before he could squeeze the trigger, Liz pulled her weapon and fired—again—and again—and again.

SIXTEEN

Liz marched into the emergency room, straight to the nurses' station, and waited impatiently for someone to acknowledge her.

"Jeremy Henderson? Adam Morgan? Sal Rizzo?"

"They're over here." Charlie joined her at the desk. "I saw you come in and I can use your help. I don't know which one of them is harder to keep down. I'm ready to insist on restraints."

The nurse laughed. "She's right. It's been a difficult few hours. They want out of here. Which is what I'm doing right now—typing up their discharge instructions. They should be ready to leave in just a few more minutes.

"Thanks."

Liz entered the room indicated and pulled back the curtains between the gurneys. Jeremy spotted her first.

"Lizzie. Jeremy needs Lizzie."

Liz gathered Jeremy in a tight hug. "Lizzie needs Jeremy, too." She ruffled the child's hair.

"About time you got here," Adam grumbled, and glowered like a bear with a thorn in his paw. "Nobody here would tell me anything. I didn't know where you went or if you were okay."

Liz laughed. The sound surprised her. She'd been laughing more and more the past few weeks. If she wasn't careful, people might mistake her for the perpetually happy Charlie.

She perched her hip on the edge of his bed and clasped his hand in hers.

"I'm told doctors make the worst patients. Are you trying to live up to that reputation?" She ignored his under-the-breath muttering and tilted her head toward Jeremy. "What do you think, Jeremy? Dr. Adam has bandages over both of his eyes this time. Think he can wiggle them like eyebrows?"

Liz knew Jeremy wouldn't understand that she was making a joke but couldn't resist. She laughed out loud when he said, "No bandages. Jeremy likes eyebrows on Dr. Adam."

"Me, too, sweetheart."

She gathered Jeremy in her arms, sat back down on a metal stool with wheels and rolled both of them a few feet past Adam. She pulled back the curtain separating Sal from the rest of them. She was surprised to see Charlie already standing on the other side of his bed. She couldn't be sure but she thought she'd caught a little hand holding going on before Charlie took a step back. At least, she'd hoped she had.

She'd thought she'd picked up a vibe between them at the barbecue and, now that she thought about it, Charlie had seemed to gravitate to Sal each shift or visit to the house.

Charlie and Sal.

Liz thought if she smiled any wider it wouldn't fit her face. She would hate to lose Sal as her right-hand man. But the thought of her two best friends building a relationship together? How wonderful was that?

"You could have called or sent a message or something. You've been gone for hours." Sal's glowering expression warmed her heart.

"I've had to take care of a few things."

"'Things'?" Sal raised an eyebrow.

"More important things than us?" Adam crossed his arms and gave her his fiercest glare.

Liz and Charlie looked at each other, shrugged and laughed some more. Sometimes men were simply taller boys.

"Let's get everyone home. We'll have plenty of time to talk later."

"Home. Jeremy wants to go home, Lizzie."

Liz held the boy against her heart. She'd never known it was possible to love a child as much as she loved this child. She offered a silent prayer of thanksgiving to the One who had brought them all together and protected them through the storms.

A week later, the four adults were gathered in Adam's backyard, lounging in chairs, nursing iced teas and enjoying the welcome stillness of the night. Crickets and frogs softly serenaded them. Candlelight flickered on the tabletops. The patio lights, the floodlight on the pond fountain, and the hanging lanterns along the brick pathways illuminated the darkness.

Jeremy was sound asleep upstairs with Rerun sprawled across him. The dog's bullet wound had not hit any vital organs. A few sutures, a thick bandage, some pain pills and Rerun was good to go. People said that dogs didn't have expressions, but Liz didn't believe it. She'd never forget the pure joy on both their faces when boy and dog were reunited.

Charlie held up the remnants of Jeremy's teddy bear. "Well, Rerun won this battle." She plucked out the few pieces of stuffing still visible in the toy. "This bear has bit the dust. I'm throwing it away while Jeremy's sleeping."

"At least we understand now why the dog kept trying to destroy it." Adam sipped his iced tea before continuing. "Who would have thought that Dave hid a flash drive inside the bear?"

Liz shrugged. "He probably thought it would be the last place Tom Miller would look for it and he was right."

"Rerun connected Miller's scent from the night of the attempted kidnapping to the bear. That's why he kept trying to pull it away from Jeremy." Charlie, who was sitting on the arm of the Adirondack chair Sal sat in, grinned. "I raise smart dogs, don't I?"

Sal looked up at her and flashed those white teeth in a broad grin meant just for her before he looked over at Adam and Liz.

"The flash drive proved that Tom Miller killed the drug dealer. Henderson must have stumbled upon the picture the snitch was trying to blackmail Tom with when he was installing our new software, saved it to a drive and took it home until he could decide exactly what he was looking at and what he should do about it."

"I still don't understand why he didn't come to me right away," Liz said.

"Hey, the guy had a picture of one of our cops killing a man that had been splashed across the newspaper as an unsolved homicide. He probably was scared. Bet the poor guy didn't know who to trust."

"Thank God Henderson did take it home." Adam looked directly at Liz. "That drive confirmed Sal's innocence. He might have been sitting behind bars tonight instead of here with friends enjoying conversation and tea."

"I'm so sorry, Sal." Liz saw a flash of pain in his eyes but knew that's all it was—just a flash. Sal had a keen intellect. He'd been able to take a look at the circumstantial evidence compiled against him and understood why Liz was going to arrest him.

"Hey, I get it. If the shoe was on the other foot, I would have had to do the same thing."

Charlie casually put her arm along the top of Sal's chair. "I haven't figured out why you ran out of the station. You didn't know Liz was going to arrest you."

"No. But I knew something was up. She wasn't acting like Liz."

Liz interrupted. "At least you noticed how difficult it was for me. I could barely entertain the idea that you might be our killer. But I still had to do my job."

Sal gave a mock salute with his glass. "Understand, boss. Really, I get it."

"So?" Charlie asked again. "Why'd you run?"

"It was a coincidence—"

"God-incidence. There's no such thing as a coincidence." Charlie playfully poked his shoulder.

"Okay, God-incidence."

Liz almost choked on her iced tea. Sal acknowledging the possibility that God might have had a hand in things? She'd prayed so hard over the years for Sal to come to the Lord. Listening to him now shocked her to her core. Her eyes filled with tears. God used people, places and things for His good. This time He'd paired Sal with a woman who would change his life…both this life and the next.

"I told you that I had a hunch I was following up on." He looked over at Liz and she nodded. "Well, I'd just about finished my interview with Grimes. It went nowhere and I was pretty sure his crime was adultery, not murder. I was cutting him loose when I got a text message from one of my snitches. He was cutting his losses and skipping town. He agreed to meet me if I came before his bus left."

"He's the one who told you about Miller?" Adam's voice made his words a question rather than a statement.

"Yeah. He had told me a week before that word on the street was that a cop killed the dealer but he didn't have any hard-core evidence. I greased his palm with a little green and told him to find something solid. When I met him at the station, he gave me Miller's name—and the name of the other guy in the alley that night who'd decided to try to blackmail Tom."

"So, if this guy witnessed the murder and tried to blackmail Tom, then why did he come forward as Tom's snitch and testify against you?" Adam crossed his ankle over his knee. "That was taking a pretty big chance for a junkie. I'm surprised he did it."

"I'm not. The guy didn't really have a choice. Tom promised him immunity and gave him enough money to disappear. What other choice did he have? He knew Tom would kill him if he didn't do what he was told."

"I can't believe Tom did all of this." Liz leaned forward and rested her arms on her thighs. "Drug addict? Murderer?" She shook her head. "I can't wrap my mind around it all. My father and Tom had been the macho guys that ran this town with an iron hand. They had no tolerance or empathy for any kind of addiction."

"I think it was a combination of things, boss. I know he never said anything to you but he was bent out of shape when you got elected sheriff. He always assumed when your father left office that he'd be next in line."

"I understand. I tolerated his insubordination and attitude because of it." Liz shook her head. "I've always known he resented my position for that reason and also because I was a woman. Men in his position, from his generation, aren't used to women in the workforce, let alone having them be their boss." She leaned back in her chair. "But drugs? When did that start?"

"After Ellie died." Sal finished off his tea. "My snitch gave me the dates when he first started making buys. I guess nine months ago when he lost his wife, who we both know waited on him hand and foot, that house must have seemed pretty lonely."

"But drugs?" Liz still struggled with the idea.

"I'm sure he didn't expect to get addicted. None of my patients ever do." Adam sighed. "He probably was out drinking one night. He was lonely…bored maybe… probably a bit curious and decided to give it a try and see what all the fuss was about. I don't condone it but I see it all the time and understand how it could happen."

Liz reached up and pulled the band off her ponytail. "I can even follow Tom's crazy logic. The drug dealer murder sounds like it was self-defense. He shouldn't have tried to cover it up, but he knew his addiction would be exposed. He might have gotten away with it if the blackmail hadn't started. He just kept digging a bigger and bigger hole."

She ran her fingers through her hair, let it fall freely down her back, and tried to ignore the feel of Adam's eyes watching her every move.

"But everything that followed…the Henderson murders…shooting out the tires of my car…trying to kidnap Jeremy…framing you…the car bomb." She held her head in her hands. "This was all such a nightmare."

Sal stood up. "Yeah, but it's over now. The bad guy's gone. The good guys reign." He laced his fingers with Charlie's. "I think I'm going to call it a night. Charlie's leaving for home tomorrow and we have some talking to do before she goes."

"Talking about what, Sal?" Liz couldn't keep the teasing note out of her voice.

"She's going to train a police dog for me."

"That so?" Liz's smile widened. "All the way in Montana? A dog for you here in Country Corners?"

Sal looked at her and when he did she read it all in his eyes—his blossoming love for Charlie, his dread about telling Liz he was leaving. But he would be leaving, no doubt.

Liz smiled at him. She'd miss Sal. But she knew this was the best thing that had ever happened to him. He was going to Montana. He would find a new life, a new love and a personal relationship with the Lord. She could never want anything other than that for her best friend.

"I want your gold necklace when you leave," Liz said.

He shot her a puzzled expression. That she'd figured out what he'd intended shouldn't have been a surprise. After all, she was the sheriff. But she knew her request for his necklace threw him.

"That's a macho playboy necklace, Sal. You don't

need it anymore. When you leave, I'm going to give it to Paul."

All four of them laughed—and the sound on the night air was healing and good.

"You got it, boss. Sounds like a great idea." He waved and went inside with a blushing Charlie.

Liz put her head against the back of her Adirondack chair and sighed.

Adam reached over and grasped her hand. "You handled that well. I know how hard it will be to see Sal leave."

Liz sent a gentle smile his way. "Not really. My best friend is getting together with my newest best friend. That sounds like a win-win situation to me."

"Lizzie Bradford, you are full of surprises tonight."

She tilted her head so she could look him in the eye. "What surprises?"

"You let your hair down even though you are still in uniform."

"True. Have you noticed that Jeremy hasn't been screaming bloody murder anymore when he sees me in my uniform? Do you think he's starting to adjust to the sight of them?"

"Yes. I think he's seen enough uniforms in the past three weeks that he is starting to equate them with people who help him and who love him."

She drew a breath. He knew her so well. She couldn't hide her feelings from him anymore—and she didn't want to.

"You're right. I do love him." She shifted in her seat. Only the arms of their chairs separated them. "Now that Jeremy is safe, there's no reason he can't remain here in Country Corners. The morning after Tom was killed,

I applied to be Jeremy's foster mother...while I wait to see if I am approved to adopt him."

Adam smiled. The knowing look in his eyes told her he wasn't surprised at this announcement.

"You'll make a wonderful mother, Lizzie."

"Thank you. Coming from you that means a lot."

"You've done remarkably well learning how to nurture an autistic child. I have no doubt you'll continue to learn and grow as you raise Jeremy to be an awesome adult someday."

He got out of his chair and moved toward her. He knelt on one knee so he could look directly in her eyes.

"I'd like to be there for you, Lizzie.... If you'll let me."

Her heart skipped a beat and butterflies danced in her stomach.

"I'll be happy for your professional input. You've made remarkable progress with Jeremy. He adores you."

"How about his new mama? How does she feel about me?"

Her heart didn't skip a beat this time— It stopped beating all together.

"Adam...what we had fifteen years ago...life's different now... I'm different."

He clasped her fingers and gently stroked the back of her hand with his thumb.

"You're right. You've changed. You've become stronger, independent and confident. You aren't striving to please people at the cost of your own happiness or looking for love from people incapable of giving it. You have discovered your worth, your place in God's heart and you beam with it. You are kind and loving and gifted. But one thing hasn't changed, Lizzie." He leaned in closer, his lips mere inches from hers. "Your smile still lights up a room like the sun on a spring day."

Her throat constricted and her eyes misted with joy. He couldn't have said anything nicer to her—until he spoke again.

"I've missed your smile. I don't want to spend another day of my life without seeing that sunshine, without feeling its warmth on my face. Please forgive me for leaving, Lizzie. I know I don't deserve a second chance, but I'm on my knee asking you for one.

"I love you, Lizzie Bradford. I've loved you since I tossed mud at you in kindergarten. I'm praying that you love me, too."

Liz couldn't hide behind her protective armor anymore. Jeremy had found the first crack. Then Charlie and Sal and Adam and even Rerun had chipped away until the cold, hard emptiness inside her chest was gone and more love than she could express filled her being.

Yes, love requires trust and faith. It requires compromise and forgiveness. It requires risk.

And, yes, a person could get hurt.

But not loving…

God never intended people to be so afraid of being hurt that they closed off emotionally to the possibility of love at all. God declared it was not good for man to be alone…or woman. How ironic that the man God sent to teach her that lesson carried the name Adam.

She smiled into his eyes.

Adam withdrew a small platinum ring with a tiny diamond in the middle.

"I bought this for you fifteen years ago. It was the best an eighteen-year-old boy could afford. But I never gave it to you. I ran away."

"You've kept it all these years?"

"I could never get rid of it. In my mind and my heart this ring always belonged to you."

He slid the ring on her *right* hand. The tiny diamond sparkled in the candlelight.

"I'm giving this to you now as a promise ring. I promise to prove to you I am worth the risk. You can open your heart to me, Lizzie. I will never let you down again."

He kissed the back of her hand.

"And I promise to give you the time you need to come to that conclusion yourself—a week, a month, a year? Whatever you need. I'm not going anywhere. I'm going to be right here, Lizzie, loving you."

He kissed her chin, her cheek and then lowered his head to claim her lips with his own. The taste of his lips, the feel of his breath, the warm, passionate kisses that followed melted away once and for all any wall, any coldness, any barrier she had ever built around her heart. She was basking in love and joy.

Adam looked deeply into her eyes.

"I promise—when you're ready—if you can find it in your heart to love me back, that I will build a life with you and Jeremy. We will fill our home with children—lots of children—our own and those others have discarded who need us. We will place God as the foundation of our life together. We will fill our home with love and laughter and happiness."

Even in the candlelight, he couldn't hide the glistening in his eyes.

"And I promise that the ring I slip on your *left* hand will be considerably larger than this puny little promise ring."

Liz laughed out loud and playfully swatted at him.

His gaze deepened in intensity and his voice trembled with emotion.

"I promise, Lizzie…my heart…my life…my love… forever and always…when you are ready to receive them."

Liz tenderly cupped his face with her hand and smiled. She leaned forward and kissed him…tenderly… then passionately. When the kiss ended she raised her eyes.

"I'm ready now, Adam. Forever and always…. I promise."

* * * * *

COMING NEXT MONTH
from Love Inspired® Suspense
AVAILABLE SEPTEMBER 4, 2012

NAVY SEAL RESCUER
Heroes for Hire
Shirlee McCoy

Despite a prison term for crimes she didn't commit, someone still thinks Catherine Miller deserves punishment. Can former navy SEAL Darius Osborne keep her safe?

STANDING GUARD
The Defenders
Valerie Hansen

A traumatized widow and child wrench Thad Pearson's heart. But tracking down the culprit wrecking Lindy Southerland's life could land Thad *and* Lindy in more danger.

THE MISSING MONARCH
Reclaiming the Crown
Rachelle McCalla

When his estranged wife and young son are threatened, Crown Prince Thaddeus must choose between defending the country he loves...and saving the woman he never could forget.

RICOCHET
Christy Barritt

Working at Camp Hope Springs only brings Molly Hamilton trouble, starting with her ex becoming her boss, and followed by dark secrets that put them both at risk.

LISCNM0812

REQUEST YOUR FREE BOOKS!

2 FREE RIVETING INSPIRATIONAL NOVELS
PLUS 2 FREE MYSTERY GIFTS

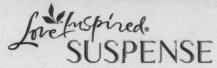

Love Inspired®
SUSPENSE

*When three bachelors arrive on Regina Nash's doorstep,
her entire world is turned upside down.*

*Read on for a sneak peek of HANDPICKED HUSBAND
by Winnie Griggs.*

Available September 2012 from Love Inspired® Historical.

Grandfather was trying to play matchmaker!

Regina's thoughts raced, skittering in several directions
at once.

How *could* he? This was a disaster. It was too manipula-
tive even for a schemer like her grandfather.

Didn't he know that if she'd *wanted* a husband, she could
have landed one a long time ago? Didn't he trust her to raise
her nephew, Jack, properly on her own?

Reggie forced herself to relax her grip on her grandfather's letter, commanded her racing pulse to slow.

She continued reading. A paragraph snagged her attention. Grandfather was *bribing* them to court her! They
would each get a nice little prize for their part in this farce.

How could Grandfather humiliate her this way?

She barely had time to absorb that when she got her next
little jolt. Adam Barr was *not* one of her suitors after all.
Instead, he'd come as her grandfather's agent.

Grandfather had tasked Adam with escorting her "beaus"
to Texas, making sure everyone understood the rules of the
game and then seeing that the rules were followed.

It was also his job to carry Jack back to Philadelphia
if she balked at the judge's terms. Her grandfather would
then pick out a suitable boarding school for the boy— rob-
bing her of even the opportunity to share a home with him
in Philadelphia.

Reggie cast a quick glance Adam's way, and swallowed hard. She had no doubt he would carry out his orders right down to the letter.

No! That would *not* happen. Even if it meant she had to face a forced wedding, she wouldn't let Jack be taken from her.

Will Regina find a way to outsmart her grandfather or will she fall in love with one of the bachelors?

Don't miss HANDPICKED HUSBAND by Winnie Griggs.

Available September 2012
wherever Love Inspired® Historical books are sold!

SHLIHEXP0912

◂—TEXAS TWINS—▸

Follow the adventure of two sets of twins who are torn apart by family secrets and learn to find their way home.

Her Surprise Sister by Marta Perry
July 2012

Mirror Image Bride by Barbara McMahon
August 2012

Carbon Copy Cowboy by Arlene James
September 2012

Look-Alike Lawman by Glynna Kaye
October 2012

The Soldier's Newfound Family
by Kathryn Springer
November 2012

Reunited for the Holidays
by Jillian Hart
December 2012

*Available wherever
books are sold.*

www.LoveInspiredBooks.com

LICONT0912